She called me her 'best friend'

By

Landy Victor

 New Generation Publishing

Dedicated to –

*Domingos Macosso, Victoria Macosso and Faithero
Macosso.*

*Thanks to Domingos Macosso, who has encouraged me
to write this book and has financed its publication. This
book is a great example of what can happen in one's
life at one time or another. The book is a good lesson
on who to take on board as a friend.*

Disclaimer

All the words in this book are my own. The book is all my own work and you will not find these words in any other book. Any resemblance to actual events, places or people, whether living or dead, is entirely coincidental.

I did nothing to her ... I mean I have never wronged her ... Believe me when I tell you that I did absolutely nothing to her.

Contents

Chapter 1

Beginning 2008, London Borough of Hillingdon
(United Kingdom)

I met her on several occasions, at times at the local park, sometimes at TK Maxx, but mostly at Asda. She stared at me like we had met before. She later told me how she had been desperate to be my friend.

The first time we spoke was the nineteenth time we saw each other. Again it was at TK Maxx. I remember it was 19 May 2008 because it was the same day I took a pregnancy test.

She said, "Have we met before?"

"I don't think so," I answered.

"I've seen you several times at the shops," she said.

"Well, maybe … eh, it's just that I don't pay too much attention to the number of people I see every day."

"I see … Anyway your beauty has always attracted me to talk to you since the first time I saw you at Asda doing shopping. You were wearing white trousers and a yellow top. I thought that it would have been very embarrassing had I come to ask for your friendship at that particular time, since we didn't know each other; but I thought that today could be the only time to talk to you, because I believe that it's by talking to somebody that you get to be their friend."

"Very true," I replied.

"My name is Naomi," she said.

"My name is Janet."

"Could we be friends?"

"Mmm, yes – on the condition that you stop staring at me like you have seen a ghost, because it's not very funny."

"Sorry about that, but it is just that you are very pretty and I like you and I would love to be your friend."

"Fine, and thanks for the compliment. See you some other time."

As I was just about to go, she stopped me.

"Oh, please, wait," she said. "Can I have your number? I mean so we can keep in touch."

"Wait a minute – are you sort of a lesbian? Sorry to ask, but I have to know … I mean, who are you?"

"Oh, no, I am not," she answered. "Eh-eh-eh no, I just want to be friends. Seriously – nothing else but just friends. You look kind and lovely."

We exchanged mobile numbers and she made a promise to give me a call that evening.

In the evening, when I saw my phone ringing with a number that wasn't registered in my contact list, I thought that it would be her. I didn't save her number on my phone because I wasn't interested in the idea of being her friend.

When I picked up, a voice said, "Hello, Janet."

"Hello. To whom am I speaking please?"

"To Naomi. Didn't you save my number earlier on when we exchanged numbers?"

"Oh, I am so sorry. I completely forgot to save your number, but never mind – I will do that later. So how are you, dear?"

"Oh, I am fine, thank you. Just called as I promised … So what are you doing now?"

"Oh, I am just writing a short story."

"Oh, you write!"

"Yes, I do, but I am not a qualified writer yet – hopefully in the future."

"That's very clever of you. So what do you write?"

"Well, poems and short stories, nothing much

really."

"Interesting. What are you writing now?"

"I am writing a short story called *The Solution Road*."

"Can you tell me a bit about the story?"

"I am afraid I can't, because my stories are always kept private to myself."

"OK, ha-ha, so that nobody copies them, right?"

"Exactly. It's a good way of protecting my work."

"Yeah, right … By the way, how old are you, Janet?"

"I am twenty two. Why do you ask?"

"Oh, nothing, just to know. Me, I am twenty-seven years old and in a relationship with a stupid guy. He's always driving me crazy. To be honest with you, I have had enough of this relationship."

"Really?"

"He has cheated on me again, but the most painful part of it is that he has done it this time with my best friend. Can you imagine?"

"Oh, sorry, mmm, so what are you going to do about it?"

"That is it! I don't know what to do. I really don't know. Seriously, I really need help this time. I have had enough with him … Any advice from you, please?"

"Me … Well … What can I say? I mean, if he really loves you and wants things to go well between you guys, he will think of changing, so talk to him and sort things out between you."

"I have tried that several times."

"Then ask him why he does that. I mean, what makes him react that way?"

"I tried that too, and he said he just can't help himself whenever he sees a sexy woman."

"Oh, I see. But that doesn't sound right, because I believe that it's not every sexy woman that goes on sleeping around with men. Some women look good just because they like looking good and not to be a sex image to some men. Maybe it's just him, like he said, who likes women, or perhaps there is something else he does not want to tell you."

"He is so cute, Janet. And because he's so cute he believes he can have any woman he wants."

"So he's very confident in himself."

"He is too confident. He doesn't even care about me the way I care about him. Or how I feel when he cheats."

"Really …"

"He's always making friends with girls."

"And you are jealous?"

"Yes, I am jealous – he likes women so much."

"OK. Well, from what we have discussed so far, I don't see how I can provide you with any further advice. Just talk some sense into him, make things work out."

"And you know what? The other day I caught him in his room sleeping with two girls at the same time."

"That's not too decent of a man."

"And all he could do was chase me out of his flat."

Naomi went on and on about this guy. I became bored with the topic, as there was no need to tell me all that. Instead there was a need for a solution to her problem. I had to stop her, so I said, "Naomi, my husband is calling me. Let me go – we will catch up tomorrow."

"OK then, thanks for your time," she responded.

"You are welcome, dear. Bye."

I checked the call duration: an hour and fifteen minutes. I wasn't happy with myself, as I should have got off the phone earlier and done something useful with my time. I guess I didn't want to embarrass her for the very first time. To be honest, I wasn't interested in her friendship.

A few minutes later, my husband returned from work. I always covered him with kisses when he got home to help him take his busy mind off work, and then I set the table for him to have his dinner while he took his shower.

He came down and sat at the table around 7 p.m.

"So how was your day, John, busy as always?"

"Very busy. I had to finish off a case and send it off to the Home Office. I am glad I was able to finish it."

"That's good news."

"And you, sugar, how was your day?"

"Not too bad. Just went to TK Maxx. I was looking for a nice pair of shoes as a gift for Stacey for her birthday."

"How is she, Stacey?"

"She's very fine. She's just busy shopping for her birthday party."

"And did you manage to get something for her?"

"Yes, I did, after a long round of searching."

"Good news for you, too. Before I forget, the food is very delicious as usual."

"You are welcome, honey. You need to be thanking my mum for making your wife a very good cook and a good wife."

"I will always thank her because she did a very perfect job on you."

We both laughed.

"Honey," I said, "I almost forgot to tell you. There is this lady I spoke with today. We have seen each other on different occasions when I have been out shopping. The first time I saw her was at Asda, and you wouldn't believe the way she was staring at me. It was like we had met before, but I had no idea who she was. Today I met her again in TK Maxx, and this time she had the courage to speak to me. Can you imagine that she told me that she liked me and wanted to be my friend … that I am so pretty and I have a great smile … She went on and on. In short, she wants to be my friend. I was so shocked when she told me all this and even asked her whether she was a lesbian, and she was like, 'Eh-eh-eh, no, I just like you.'"

"You are not serious, are you?"

"Honey, I am serious. If somebody had told me that things like this happen, I wouldn't have believed them. But trust me, she even asked me for my number, and I gave it to her."

"Hey, hey, no – never do such a thing again. You don't know somebody – you don't give them any contact of yours, particularly when the person has been doing some sort of what I would call 'hunting you'. I am not happy with you on this one."

"Oh, I am sorry, honey."

"Let it be the last time you do such a thing. Get to know the person first before you start thinking of giving them your number."

"I promise you it won't happen again. I am truly sorry. Anyway, not to spoil your mood, let me finish up with some good news – that is, if you are still interested in hearing further from me?"

"Go on, I am all ears."

"I am pregnant."

"It's a joke! Are you serious, or are you just pulling my leg?"

"Seriously, I am pregnant. Remember when I told you about the nausea and tiredness I have been having lately? I thought it would be good if I took a pregnancy test, and the result came out positive. So I have booked an appointment with the doctor."

"You have got me on this one. This is great news. I am going to be a father … Listen, come, let's dance to this."

"No, wait – not until we have finished eating."

"Oh, please, let's dance!"

"No, finish your food first."

"Alright, alright … My God. From today on we have to start thinking and preparing for all the things that our dear prince or princess will need. Everything must be ready as we welcome him. Alleluia! I am going to be a father … la-la-la-la … a father, la-la-la-la."

"Easy, honey, and finish your food."

"You can't tell how excited I am, can you? I am going to start a family, woman! And family is the most important thing in the whole wide world. So many things will change. I will be coming back home from work knowing that I have a lovely wife and child waiting for me. I mean, it makes me happier and complete. Children are gifts from God and I wouldn't want to be anywhere else and have anything else but a good home with a beautiful family."

"That's so sweet of you, honey."

"You are the sweetest thing in my life. What would I ever do without you, my sugar?"

"You with that word 'sugar' all the time."

"Because you are the sugar in my cup of tea. Oh, didn't you know?"

"I now know."

"Oh, come on, you are just pretending as if you didn't know. You just want me to be saying it over and over again … Well, I will tell you more. You know the song *Sugar, Sugar* by the Archies?"

"Yeah."

"That song describes what you mean to me. *Sugar, sugar – you are my candy girl, and you got me wanting you … I just can't believe the loveliness of loving you … I just can't believe the wonder of this feeling, too … Oh, sugar, sugar …*"

"Well, thank you for singing, honey."

"And you – what is all this 'honey' about all the time? Does it have a song too?"

"Ha-ha, yes it does. Do you know the song *Honey, Honey* by ABBA? That song also describes what you mean to me."

"I can't wait for us to dance to both these songs."

"Patience, my husband, we will. By the way, you can sing."

"Don't mock me."

"No, seriously, you tried."

"I won't take that as a compliment."

"Ha-ha-ha. Oh, I thank God that I am a very happy wife. I have a good husband, and I wouldn't have been any happier with any other man but you."

"Really …"

"Yes, honey, really."

"Well, thank you for confirming that to me. And you are the best woman I have ever had. You are so wonderful and I know how lucky I am to have you."

"And that's so sweet of you. Anyway, you know there is one thing we keep on doing that we both know we shouldn't be doing."

"I know what it is."

"And what is that?"

"You're not supposed to talk when you eat at the table. But you started this time."

"OK, OK, I take the blame. But no more talking now."

"Just one more thing please before I zip my mouth."

"What again?"

"I love you."

"I love you, too," I said with a smooth tone of voice.

Chapter 2

The next morning when I woke up I saw that my husband had left a red rose next to my pillow. As soon as I set my eyes on it, it was like the whole world belonged to me. I loved my life and I was a very happy wife. This flower inspired me to write another poem for my book, which I called *Tips On How to Live a Successful Life*, so I quickly grabbed a pen and my notebook. I was very happy with the way my book was progressing, and I couldn't wait to publish it. I had always dreamt of being a writer, and I hoped to fulfil this dream one day. I started writing poems and short stories when I was a little girl. I worked so hard when I was young. I was twenty one when I got married and was in my last year at university. To be honest I had not had the normal life of a young lady. I would rather spend time reading, observing nature and watching the news than going to parties, but I loved going to places such as restaurants, museums and the cinema. After graduation I couldn't get a job related to my politics and journalism degree because of my lack of experience within the field, so I thought that volunteering in the meantime was the best thing to do. At first I volunteered with an Adult Learning Centre where I was an Information and Communications Technology (ICT) assistant to the tutor. Later my husband told me to volunteer with his law firm and I told him I would think about it. This was what I wrote on 20 May 2008:

Victory is a mystery that may happen in a short period of time just as it may take a long period of time.
Victory comes in years, months, days, hours or minutes,

as it might come in seconds.
Victory is when you win a battle.
Victory is when all power comes back to you – that of
your adversaries and that which you lost in the battle.
Victory comes to those who are not hypocrites.
Victory comes to those who are humble.
Victory comes to those who never give up.
Victory comes to those who are true in their heart.
Victory comes to those who, in their heart, accept
humiliation for the cause they are fighting.

After I had finished writing this I had a bath, ate breakfast, and then left home for the centre.

The students at the centre loved me so much and always wanted me to come every Tuesday; they told me that I was really good at teaching them and could be a very good lecturer in the future.

That evening, on my way back home from the centre, I received a phone call from my husband asking me whether he should pick me up. I said no, I was OK to take the bus. It was already 6 p.m. At the bus stop, as I waited for the bus, there was a young lady waiting for it too. This lady started staring at me. I thought to myself, *Not again.*

She said, "You are very pretty."

"Thanks," I replied.

"My name is Zulu. I just arrived in the UK a year ago and I am from Africa."

I said, "Nice to meet you, Zulu."

The bus arrived. I got on and she did, too. I took a seat and she sat next to me.

"What's your name, if I may ask?" she said.

"My name is Janet."

"Nice name."

"Thank you, Zulu."

"Oh, you remembered my name. Most people don't

after I have just told them my name."

I remained silent and just gave her a smile.

"Wow! What a lovely and beautiful smile you have!"

"Thanks again, Zulu."

"Could we be friends?"

"I guess we already are friends, Zulu."

"Thank you, Janet. Is it possible for me to have your phone number?"

I hesitated before answering her, because I had made a promise to my husband not to repeat the same scenario again. I decided to give her one of my alternative email addresses. "Zulu, my phone is having problems at the moment and I don't know my number, but I will give you my email address so you can email me anytime."

"Sure, that's fine," she said.

I can't believe that I have just told a lie, I thought. *Oh, Heavenly Father, may you forgive me for this.*

"So what brought you to the UK?" I asked Zulu.

"My father lives here, so I joined him."

"I see."

"But it's been very hard for me to make friends with people because they find me too unattractive to be their friend."

"Who told you that you were not attractive?"

"Well, that is what most of them say. They say that I am ugly. I am so lame."

"Zulu, there is no ugly person in the world. You have to believe in yourself and not in what people tell you. Do you believe in that yourself?"

"Well … I don't know. Maybe. I mean, I am very dark skinned, not highly educated. My father left for the UK when I was only two years old. My mum remarried and forced me to stay with my grandmother because her new husband didn't want to have me, so I grew up with my grandmother. I dropped out of school at eleven years old because we had no money to pay my school fees. I later joined my grandmother, who was selling peanuts at the local market, until the good news about my father came around. Today I am twenty-one years old, but I guess I may manage to further my education, though time is flying. All my hopes lie in the future. But some people believe that I cannot catch up with the education I have missed."

"Oh yes you can, Zulu! Firstly, let me tell you that you are pretty and I find you very attractive. You have nice beautiful dark skin. Secondly, you have said it yourself, that 'some people believe I cannot …', meaning that those people are just one of the percentage of people that will never say, 'Yes, you can.' Zulu, there are two categories of people in this world: the **good side** and **the bad side**. So, wherever and whenever you meet deceiving people, know that they are just another percentage of the bad side, and have nothing to do with them unless they are willing to change and move on to the good side. I call these categories **'angels of the other side'**, because the question is what side does a person want to belong to, the good side or the bad side? Think about it, Zulu. If you ever decided that you wanted to belong to the good side, then, trust me, you would not be bothered about what the angels of the other side say about you, because you would already know that nothing good comes from that side. All they do is minimise to equalise, because they know that they are not fit to belong to the good side, so they want to deceive as many people as possible to get them to their level … Oh my God, I nearly missed my stop. Zulu, it was nice talking to you. Email me, OK? I have to get off now."

"Thank you so much, Janet. Bye!" she said loudly.

I got off the bus. My home was only a two-minute

walk from the bus stop, so I quickly rushed home to exercise my duty to my husband as always. When I got home, I set the table and quickly had a bath. It was very silent that evening at the table, as we promised each other that we would not talk while eating, and it was very boring, but that was the rule and we had to respect it. As soon as we finished I took the dishes to the kitchen, washed them up and rushed straight back to the living room. I joined my husband on the sofa, where we both shouted at the same time, "How was your day?" Very funny. We exchanged and exchanged stories about our day while we watched TV before going to bed.

In bed my husband told me something I really liked.

He said, "Janet, I want you to know that there are only **three moments** in life, and I want you to enjoy the second one most, because it's the most enjoyable moment of life. However, having said that, the first two moments are the most important moments of life. **The first moment** is when you are born: this moment is very important, as it determines your success in life. This is where you are born to a family and the family hold your future in their hands, so they must be well prepared to receive you as you come to them, and must continue to support you as you grow; otherwise you will not get enough support to grow as a successful child and will not have an enjoyable 'second moment'. As the child grows, the parents or parent of the child and the child himself must work hard together in order for the child to succeed. The child must be wise, respectful to its parents and listen to their good advice, and parents must know what is good for their child. This first moment determines whether the child's second moment is going to be of enjoyment or not. If this child works hard in collaboration with the parents, the child will have a bright future and a good life, resulting in an enjoyable second moment of life. But if the child does not work hard and does not collaborate with his parents/guardians, or the parents do not sufficiently support the child, he will not have an enjoyable 'second moment' of life.

"The **second moment** – or the second stage, if you like – is where the hard work has paid off: the child has a good job and a wonderful family and starts enjoying his life. This is the moment I want you to enjoy now, as it is the most beautiful moment of life.

"The **third and final moment** is when you die. When you die you are gone, but those behind you will remember you for your successful life in the sands of time (in both your first and second moments), while you die happily.

"In conclusion, putting all these three moments together, this is what they look like.

"As I come out, I can see people shouting for joy. The moment has come. I am born. They just cannot stop loving me. I know nothing yet.

"As I walk the stage, people behind me are shouting for joy. Relatives are proud of me. Friends are praising me. Enemies are burning. The moment has come. I am a man now. I have succeeded in life. This moment is mine: a special moment that will last forever. Those behind me will always feel my force and competence, as these will leave my mark on history.

"As I walk the stage, people behind me are crying. They are shouting through tears. They don't want me to go, but it's time for me to go. I have lived a happy life. Nothing can change things as they are now, because the moment has come.

"So, sugar, I want you to enjoy your life as much as you can. This is the moment of enjoyment, so you cannot miss it. OK, my sugar?"

"Honey, you are so right. Thank you. I have enjoyed

every piece of your advice. I will enjoy *my second moment of life* to the fullest!" I shouted with joy.

He then said, "Another thing I would like to tell you, sugar, is that I have worked so hard to be where I am today. I understand that you are finding it hard to get a job and you have been feeling unhappy about it lately because I am the only one who's providing for us, but don't forget that I am your husband and it is my responsibility to take care of you. I have passed through what you are going through at the moment, and I am not complaining in any way. So please stop imagining that I may one day complain – because, trust me, I will never complain about providing for my wife. And who knows what you are going to become in the future? Maybe the next great British writer," he laughed.

"I know, honey, but it's just that I have to contribute too to our living expenses. I mean, that's how it's supposed to be," I responded.

He held me close to him. "And I have told you not to worry yourself. The time will come. Take it easy. I mean, you are doing your best by volunteering, meaning you are in line to get a job one day, because the more work experience you get, the more likely you are to get a job. So you are really trying."

"Thanks, honey. It's good to hear that from you. I promise you that one day I will get a good job."

"You will indeed, because I know you will. Listen, let me give you one example – perhaps this one will help you understand clearer what I mean when I say don't worry. This example is very much linked to the *first moment of life*. In life you have to bear in mind that **it is hard to be somebody**.

"We all work very hard to become somebody and live a better life. We give all our energy to work to 'get there'. Getting there might be to arrive at a shop selling a better quality of shoe, depending upon which quality

22

you want to wear.

"Every one of us knows the size and quality of the type of shoe he wants to wear, so what we do is to work hard at getting that shoe. When and how we do that is a question to do with time. It can happen that we change our minds because, for instance, we have waited for so long that we can't afford the shoe anymore or it has become too expensive. If this is the case, we might decide to look for another shoe, but that will trouble our objectives. We might think of changing a few other things. We might change to another shop, because the new shoe might not be in the same shop as the old one. To change to another shop would be another big deal, because we have to find where it is and consider the price they offer. If we find a cheap price, that means we can buy the shoe, but when we look at the quality of the shoe we are disappointed, as we already know that the shoe will not last for long; so we may decide to keep our money and continue saving because we think of going back to the old shoe. So after we have saved enough we now make our way back to the previous shop. Once again, this is another big deal, because as we travel to get that old shoe we might find out that it has already been sold. Now we find ourselves in a world of confusion, but no matter how disappointed we are, we can find solutions to the confusion. We make decisions, we seek more energy and we get back to work, for we know it is hard to be somebody."

"What a clever brain you have, my husband. Thanks, honey. You are so sweet."

"You are welcome."

"I understand now. People work hard to be where they want to be."

"Exactly. Just as you have worked hard at university to get your degree. I am very happy that you have understood."

"I love you."

"Love you more."

Then we made love as ever before.

Friday 23 May 2008

Stacey called me the morning that she was on her way to my house to pick me up to accompany her to the hair salon as we had recently planned. She had booked an appointment with the hairdresser to get her hair done nicely before her birthday. We had some coffee and blueberry muffins at my place before we left for the salon. She wasn't really herself that day and I wasn't happy to see her that way. I wanted her to be happy because her birthday was just around the corner, and I didn't want anything unhappy to come her way, not when it was going to be her birthday soon. I knew that her bad mood was due to the same issues about her husband which she had been telling me about.

At my place, she said, "I don't understand Paul anymore. He's not changing at all about his issues of women and fashion. He has started again. Yesterday, when we both went out to finalise my birthday-party shopping, he saw one lady wearing a very short skirt and he was off again, saying, 'Stacey, why don't you like wearing short skirts?'"

"Huh. Not again."

"He has always wanted me to wear shorts or short skirts and short dresses. I mean, I don't have to wear such things to look sexy. I keep on telling him not to compare me to other women. These women he compares me to are who they are, and I am Stacey. Come on, Janet, you don't need to put on short clothes to look sexy, do you?"

"You are very correct."

"You can look sexy even in long skirts, a long dress

24

or trousers. The other day he asked me why I couldn't buy myself some red thongs and some skinny jeans. I wonder where he has seen that? Gosh, it's so annoying what he's always asking me to do. I have had it up to here now."

"But seriously, comparing your wife to another woman is not the way for a man to get what he wants from his wife. I mean, you don't know how other women are or how they treat their husbands in their homes. Whether they make their husbands their money slaves, nobody knows."

"Thank you, Janet. That is also what I have been telling him. Some women turn their husbands to wives and themselves to husbands. So it's the other way round. If you don't buy what they want you to buy for them, you have problems with them. But see me, Janet, I have never complained to my husband. I don't ask him for money or make him buy me something ..."

"Take it easy. Let me tell you one thing – you are a good wife. Don't make your husband change you for no reason at all. Most women give all their own money and that of their husbands to the 'world of fashion' and end up having no savings for themselves or their children. You don't want to be like them, do you?"

"Of course not, never in my life. But what pains me the most is that we have a mortgage to finish off, and yet he keeps on telling me to buy myself expensive fashionable clothes and accessories. Doesn't he see that he makes no sense? Janet, since we got a mortgage I have bought all my clothes in charity shops, like British Red Cross and Cancer Research. I mean, he's really hurting me."

"Of course he makes no sense. Listen, it's now left to you to make him understand this by continuing to be what you are but at an improved level. Wear your trousers and keep them fit and sexy. Continue doing your shopping in charity shops, as long as you are getting what's good for yourself. Your husband will soon come to understand the sacrifices you make for the both of you."

"Janet, come to think of it, considering my age I wouldn't want to wear short skirts. In fact, I have never worn them before in all my life."

"And don't wear them. It's not something to do with age. You just continue being who you are. Take a good look at me. I don't wear short clothes either, but my husband always says that I am sexy. I wear my trousers and long dresses, as long as they fit me properly. So, my dear, continue being who you are, and believe me your husband will come to love your own unique style of dressing. What you are is what makes you unique to other women. It is what makes the difference between you and them. So don't let your husband's issues bother you again. Find some lovely long sexy dress to wear tomorrow which you might already have in your wardrobe. Let the dress hug your body from the top all the way down, and wear some nice, beautiful heels. Trust me, he won't take his eyes off you for some other woman."

"Thank you, Janet. That's why you are the only friend I can trust. You are too young to be my friend, but your brain is up to the task. Janet, I just want my husband to be thinking of important things, like thinking of adopting children now that we are not able to have children of our own."

"Children will come, OK? Just a little more patience, and trust me you will have children of your own."

"I am not getting younger, Janet. If I start having them at a very old age, when am I going to start raising them? Tell me? Look at you – you are pregnant and very young and you have plenty of time to raise your children."

"They will come, Stacey, trust me. Keep your faith up. We had better start going now, or you will miss your appointment."

"Oh, yeah, I almost forgot. Too much on my mind. Let's go, dear."

We continued talking in her car as we went to the hairdressers. At the hairdressers Stacey had her hair cut in the style of Rihanna, short with side fringes. The hairstyle was just so stunning that I planned doing it too after I had got rid of the one I had. Stacey looked stunning. No words could explain the way her face changed to become like Rihanna the pop star. As soon as her hair was finished she told me that we should go to Debenhams. On our way to Debenhams, as soon as we entered the shopping centre, people started looking at Stacey's hair, saying "Very nice hair" and "You look like Rihanna". It was amazing to see how Stacey felt about herself. In Debenhams she bought a red, shiny, sexy, short-sleeved long dress. When she tried it on in the shop, I imagined how crazy Paul would be when he saw her wearing it. I was very happy that we were able to get back at Paul in our own way. Not doing anything stupid, but just showing him how pretty his wife was and that he should accept her with her own style. Stacey said she would wear her dress with the shiny black heels she had at home. I was very happy for her. Later we had a buffet in a Chinese restaurant. While we enjoyed our Chinese dishes Stacey told me that she had also explained her situation to a friend at work, who gave her the following advice: "If your husband has been saying these things to you, it means he is seeing another woman. You should look for some cute guy to have fun with just to get back at him. Trust me, he will change as soon as he finds out. I tried it before and it worked."

27

I couldn't believe my ears. Some people give bad advice to their friends when it comes to situations like this, but this was something else. "Do you understand the implications of what she advised you? You could be accused of committing adultery and end up divorcing."

"Don't you worry, Janet. I have already dealt with her," said Stacey.

"Stacey, marriages will always have problems. But getting back at your husband in the way your friend described would be to disgrace yourself and break your marriage."

"Thank you, Janet. That is why you are my best friend, and I must say I am happy to have a friend like you."

Saturday 24 May 2008 – Stacey's birthday party

Naomi called me early and asked me what I was up to for the day. I told her nothing, other than a friend's birthday party in the evening. She insisted that she go with me, saying that she loved going to parties. I told her that it was OK by me. Then she asked whether she could come over to my house so we could go together and I said fine.

So that evening, for the very first time, Naomi came to my house.

As she walked into my house she couldn't believe her eyes. "What a beautiful home you have, Janet!"

"Oh, thanks."

"Wow! Is it yours or your husband's?"

"My husband's."

"No wonder ..."

"Why?"

"You couldn't own a house like this for yourself, looking at your age."

"And what if I had won the lottery and become a

millionaire at the age of eighteen," I joked, "or my parents were millionaires?"

"That is *if* you had won the lottery, darling, and your parents are not millionaires ... So what does your husband do?"

"He's a solicitor."

"So is it rented, or he owns the house?"

"His own legal property."

"That's very good, girl. Smart girl. Good husband you have here. And how old is he?"

"He's ten years older than me. And what did you mean by 'smart girl'?"

"What? Is he not too old for you, looking at the age gap? You are now twenty two, right?"

"Yes, but I see nothing wrong with that. We get along so well, like we are the same age."

"Oh, babes ... You should have gotten yourself a young guy. Don't you think so?"

"Are you kidding me? Anyway, enough with the 'age gap' thing. Can we get dressed? I don't want us to be late for the party."

"Sure. By the way, what I meant by 'smart girl' was that you went for the rich. There is one thing I love about you, and that is that you are so simple and humble. I mean, looking at your home, your academic background and your husband's position in society, you could have been bold and proud – not willing to make friends with anybody unless they are middle class too."

"For your information, I am not a material lady and I am not a middle-class person. I am just me, nothing else."

"Well, you look like one."

"OK, fine."

"If I were you I would only be friends with middle-class people."

"And what's that supposed to mean? That wouldn't

be fair. Besides, are you telling me that you know all of my friends, or that it's you who's finding yourself uncomfortable with me?"

"What do you mean by that?"

"I don't know. You tell me. Because I don't get you, Naomi. Anyway, let's just start getting dressed, please."

"Fine. And sorry if I have offended you in any way. By the way, is he coming with us?"

"Who? You mean my husband?"

"Yep."

"No, he's not. He's got a lot of paperwork to catch up with in the office Monday. He'll be very busy tonight working on some of his cases."

"Oh, I see. Alright. It's all good without the old man anyway."

I shook my head. "Could you please stop calling him that?"

"Have I said something wrong again? Come on. It's just an expression."

"And who told you it's a young people's party we are going to? My husband is a very busy man and he barely has time for parties."

"People do say sometimes 'old man' or 'young man' ..."

"He's not an old man. That's what I am trying to make you understand. Simply because he's ten years older than me doesn't make him an old man."

"I didn't mean he's an old man. It's an expression I used. Don't you get it?"

"Well, never use that expression again about my husband."

"Whatever ... Fine. Give me a break!"

"By the way, why didn't you get dressed at your place?"

"I just didn't want to. I feel more excited when I get dressed at a friend's place. I love being watched when I am dressing, because I am always asking how I look."

"Alright, let's do this."

"That is it! I love that. You are now being cool."

"You are very funny, Naomi. You know that?"

We arrived at Stacey's birthday party around 7 p.m. There was a big crowd. As soon as Stacey walked into the party hall she caught everybody's attention. She was looking stunning, like twinkle-twinkle little star, the diamond in the sky. I was flushed with happiness for Stacey. I gave her a great smile and she smiled back.

Naomi whispered in my ear. "How could she dress like that on her birthday? She's not looking good. What a pity."

"Naomi," I whispered back, "please behave yourself, and do appreciate whenever you see something good."

Paul couldn't take his eyes away from his wife, not even for a second, and this made me feel even happier for Stacey. I couldn't wait to tell her myself how crazy her husband had become about her.

First I introduced Stacey and Naomi to each other. They were both happy to get to know each other. We relaxed and started to enjoy the party. An hour later Stacey blew out the candles on her birthday cake. It was really fun. There was lots of food and drink. Stacey was celebrating her thirty-fifth birthday. Naomi was really enjoying herself – walking from one side to another and dancing to her favourite tunes, leaving me alone to enjoy the food.

Later on I saw Naomi heading towards me. She came straight up to me and whispered in my ear again.

"I can't believe you," she said. "How can you have a friend who's so much older than you? She's thirty-five years old. I mean, how do you guys get along with each other? Isn't she too old to have fun with? You'd better be kidding me, Janet."

I whispered back that she should stop, because a few people were watching us and could have been thinking that we were criticising others.

The next time I saw Naomi she was flirting with some guy. She asked the guy for a dance. After the dance she asked him for his mobile number. I was a bit concerned with the way she was behaving at the party. Three hours later I felt like leaving. I left my seat and went up to where she was sitting and chatting with the same guy. I asked her if we could leave, explaining I was tired. She refused. She said her time wasn't up yet. I insisted that I had to go home, but told her that if she preferred to stay, that was OK. I then went to tell Stacey I was leaving and she gladly asked her husband to drop me off.

As we were walking out the door, Naomi said, "Are you really going?"

"Yes, dear, I am," I responded.

"Wait for me, please!" she called out. She kissed the guy on the lips, took her handbag and picked up a bottle of red wine.

As we got outside I asked Paul to drop me off first. Paul had forgotten his car keys and so went back to the party hall to get them. I used this opportunity to tell Naomi what was on my mind.

"Naomi, what do you think you were doing in there with that guy?"

"Who? Which guy?"

"The guy you kept a prisoner to yourself."

"You mean Spencer? Oh, come on. What was I doing wrong with him?"

"Don't tell me that you don't know what I am trying to bring to your attention."

"Janet, please don't be childish. What did I do

wrong with the guy? Just answer me!"

"Naomi, you had your hands all over him and this is a guy you barely know."

"Straight to your point, Janet!"

"I mean, how can you sell yourself so low to a guy just like that? He should have been the one asking you out and not the other way around."

"Are you insulting me in some way? Is it your first time seeing a lady asking a man out? You've got to be kidding me, Janet!"

"You don't need to raise your voice. I just felt that what you were doing was not decent of a lady. I mean, you should respect yourself in front of a guy."

"Shut up! Shut the fuck up, Janet! Who are you to give me lessons on morals or how to respect myself?"

"Naomi, don't get me wrong. What I am saying is never sell yourself so low to any guy like you have just done, even when you feel like you love the guy. I understand that perhaps you want the guy so bad, but is he interested in you as you are interested in him? With the way you have taken it with him, he could be thinking of taking advantage of you and that's where my problem is. I just don't want you to get hurt."

"Shut up, OK! You are so stupid! I never knew you were this stupid! Is that what they have taught you – that if you ask a guy out, that's what happens? People do bad things to you only when you let them, and what tells you that I will let him?"

"With the way you were behaving you could have easily lost control and done something stupid."

"Cut it there, OK? You are the one being stupid. Who do you think you are? Saint Mary?"

"I never said that, Naomi. OK – I am sorry if I have offended you. I was just concerned."

"Mind your own business and your old-fashioned husband. Who knows, maybe you are jealous? You have never had a cute guy before, have you?"

"Naomi, how could you say that to me? I chose my husband because of who he is on the inside and not what he is or can be on the outside. Besides, haven't I told you never to use that expression again?"

"Well, to be honest with you, your husband is not as cute as my Spencer, so maybe you are trying to get me out the way so you can have Spencer to yourself ..." She laughed. "Who knows?"

"I am very disappointed in you, Naomi. I should have listened to my heart in the first place and not made friends with you. Thank you very much."

"Oh, please keep your sorry to yourself! I hate you now!"

I decided to stay calm and listen to her go on and on. She stopped as soon as she saw Paul coming back with the car keys. Paul dropped me off first. As I got out the car, the last words I said to Naomi that night were, "Please text me to let me know you have arrived home safely. Just so that I know, because I am the one who took you out."

She didn't say anything.

I got out the car, opened the gate and then the door and walked up the stairs to the bathroom. I just wanted to have a deep bath. I couldn't stop thinking about how Naomi had disrespected me. I was still in shock. Why would she treat me that way? I was only trying to show concern.

My husband could see the bad mood in me as I got into bed. He wondered what had happened to me.

I didn't want to talk about it, but he insisted, and since we never kept anything from each other I ended up telling him. "What friend would ever shout at her fellow friend simply because she's trying to make a point? I mean, I just told Naomi that she shouldn't sell herself so low to a man she barely knows, all because she thinks he is handsome. She saw a guy at the party and started making advances towards him when he wasn't even interested in getting to know her. I later told her that she was degrading herself, but all I got in return was bad language like 'Shut up!' and 'It's none of your business'. So I am still in shock. I still can't believe her."

"You know," my husband responded, "I have always been against the idea of you making friends with this girl. To be honest with you I don't like her even though I haven't met her yet. But from the way you described her the other day I felt like there is something about her that's not very nice. Anyway, I don't want what happened between the both of you to keep you up at night. Forget about it and try to get some sleep."

But I couldn't get enough sleep that night. I kept on thinking about the incident. The next morning before leaving for work my husband asked me to grab a pen and paper. Might he have noticed that I was still unhappy?

"You said you are writing a book, right?" he said.

"Yes I am, honey. What about it?"

"OK, write this down. I want you to include this in your book."

I got my notebook and wrote down what he told me to write. What I wrote down had something to do with respect, so I gave it 'respect' as a title:

Respect

When we respect other people, it does not mean that we are afraid of them, but simply that we respect them and their opinions, so they should do the same.

If you respect people but they do not respect you, there is no point in staying friends with them. Tell them that when they learn to respect you and your opinions, that is when you will get back to them. Otherwise there is no need.

Sometimes, when other people show respect, the recipient of that respect begins to take advantage, thinking they are bigger than those who respect them. It is a false position, because if I respect you today it is because I am trying to build comprehension between your ideas and mine; you should do the same or there will be no me and you.

After my husband had left I kept on reading *Respect* back to myself and I felt much better. I felt that I wasn't being a coward by not shouting back at Naomi that night; I was just respecting myself.

A few hours later my mobile phone rang. It was Naomi. I guess I was still not in the mood to talk to her, so I decided not to pick up in case I was rude to her on the phone.

Then she texted me: *Hi Janet, I didn't mean to hurt you. It was the huge amounts of alcohol I had drunk that made me go crazy. Please forgive me.*

I forgave her. Seriously I did. But I told her that it was only on the condition that she learnt how to respect me. So I texted back: *As long as you start showing me some respect, this friendship will carry on, otherwise it's over.*

This she promised me in her second text message: *I promise you Janet that I will never ever repeat the same thing again or disrespect you in any way.*

Chapter 3

Three months passed by. I was twelve weeks pregnant. We were in August.

One morning I thought of somebody and remembered that I had not checked my alternative email address. This was an email address I gave to people I was not interested in hearing from, so I hardly ever checked my messages. But with the thoughts of this person and what we shared together at one time in mind, I became interested in finding out how she was doing. I therefore decided to check the account and see whether she had written to me. There were twenty-five messages from Zulu, the last fifteen begging me for a reply. I was very happy to hear from her, though in her messages she sounded very unhappy, like she was going through a lot. What I didn't like was that she sounded very complicated. It got me thinking that what sometimes we people don't understand is that you can't have everything you want in life simply because you want it. You must not want things that will give you only a temporary joy, and not a permanent happiness. There are things you want but that you do not need (these are things which come from the outside of a man) such as cars, fashionable clothes, holidays, etc. It is normal to want to have these because they are useful, but they are not absolutely needed at one point in time because they have to do with time. In other words, at any time if there is a good opportunity for you to have them you will definitely have them.

But there are things you must have and these are absolutely necessary because they have to do with the spirit (mind/character/personality) of a man. These things come from the inside of a man and not from the outside and are very precious to have, because most of them have nothing to do with money. That is, you cannot buy them because shops don't sell them, and they cannot be found anywhere else in the world but within yourself. These things are the only things that make a man successful in life. They include wisdom, love, patience, hope, faith, honesty, respect and hard work. Together, these absolute things become a *whole unique type of education* – one that you might not gain at government education establishments, because you can gain intelligence from government education but you do not become wise or you don't know how to respect others or you don't know how to have patience. This unique class of education, together with government education, can make a man even more perfect on the inside (in his spirit).

I was concerned about Zulu as she sounded very serious. I gathered some phrases (from her messages) which caught my attention. *They say that I am ugly. They bully me all the time ... I want to look good too. I want to be attractive to people too ... I am not able to get a job because I have no work experience and my English is not yet fluent. I need a job please! Can you help me find one? What do I do? I once heard some friends saying that they sometimes steal in shops when they need a fashionable outfit to wear for a hot evening party, but what do I do? I feel very bad about myself.*

I did not provide her with an immediate response. I thought it was wise to take my time to think about how to respond. I took a few minutes to reflect and thought of all that my parents used to tell me when I was growing up. I decided to put it all down on paper, so I got a pen and paper and started writing down the advice of my parents. When I had finished and felt ready to respond I sat back at the computer and transferred all that I had written on the piece of paper to an email. In addition to my response I included my official email. This was what I wrote:

Zulu, thank you for your messages. I am doing fine thanks. I was glad to hear from you, but I must say I am a bit concerned about what you have written. I would not want to say much, but let the following advice speak for me. My father always said:

"As you walk by, living your life, be wise. Know your purpose and go for it. Don't let anyone change your mind. Be careful as you walk – there are bad people among you. They will tell you bad things and would want you to do them so that you can be like they are. Whenever you meet these type of people run far away from them because they are like demons. They never progress. They also want you to be like them and will be the first to laugh at you, saying, 'Oh, see! We have got him into our world.' Even so, most of them dream of getting out of that world one day, while they would leave you alone there, saying 'If only I had known'. Know that good and bad both exist. There are some people made to destroy while others are made to save. It is now up to you to decide on which side you want to belong.

"As you live your life, don't ask others how they work life out, because they will never tell you the truth about how they do their things. Don't compare yourself to others or to what they do or how they look. Be proud of what you are. Stay what you are and do what you can do best. Never form relationships with people because of interests such as money, looks or whatever. And do not think that every person you see who looks good really is good. Someone may well look good on the outside but not be good on the inside.

"Most people do bad things to get what they want. Most people spend their money only on themselves and don't like sharing it with family, which gives them the

opportunity to really look after themselves. But you, my daughter, whenever you have little, you always share it with family; and God, who sees what you do, will surely bless you. Be proud of who and what you are.

"You do not do bad things to get what you want. You do good things to get what you want. It was once said that a little lie can lead to success, but I tell you, my daughter, that too many lies will lead you to your downfall. A bad person continues to do bad, be it in his own interest or in the interest of other bad people. But a good person learns from his mistakes and, when he notices that the route he is on leads him to doing bad, turns back to where he started and seeks a good route to take him to his destination. You do not enchain a bad thing. You make a bad thing good.

"Be decisive, as it will help you make decisions one time and move on. If you don't want something then decide not to have it. If you don't want to do something, then don't do it. Stay firm and stand by your decisions. What your heart says about something in the first place is the right position to stand by. Being decisive will help you avoid making mistakes in life.

"Bad people are used to their lives and they know that they are already destroyed, but before they go to hell they want to make you go with them. Do not believe that you know who they are just because you frequently share conversations with them. They will be good to you. They will give you food and tell you secrets just so that you will trust them, but you must never trust them, never follow them or listen to their advice. They will do all this just because they want to know your secrets so that they can have the opportunity to destroy you.

"Whenever bad people come to you and say, 'Please, dear, do come with us,' you should respond with, 'Sorry, dear, I am busy.' But in your heart you

should know that you would never be friends with such
people. Advice or information from a good-hearted
person can be reliable and truthful, but advice from a
bad-hearted person is full of deceit and jealousy. It's
like poison. Whenever they judge you, say lies about
you or criticise you, do not bother yourself, because
they do this to minimise you so as to bring you down to
their level. They know that you shine like a star, and
therefore they will try their hardest to put that bright
light out. But you must not tremble or fear; you must
continue being that good girl that you are, and if you
do your light will shine even as bright as the stars in
the sky. If they talk behind your back, forget it and
forget about them. But if they criticise you face to face,
then you must tell them what they need to hear. Tell
them: 'When will you cut the dirty grass that surrounds
your houses? Can you not see that your houses look so
dirty to people who pass by? Yet you want to cut mine,
which is already neat. You make no sense.'"

Later in the evening, when I checked my official
email address before going to bed, there were two
messages from Zulu, the first one thanking me for my
response, and the second one saying that my advice
was really of help to her. She was able to discipline
herself, but it was only for a while; as soon as she saw
her other friends dressing all sexy for a party, she
started to panic again. I then came to understand that
Zulu was breaking into pieces in her spirit. I thought
that I had to get those pieces back together before they
fell away, so I replied and asked her if she would be
interested in going out for lunch at a restaurant over the
weekend.

The next morning I had an appointment at the
hospital. I was twelve weeks pregnant and I had to
attend my first ultrasound scan. Everything went well at
the hospital. John joined me before I had the scan. It

was a very significant moment in our lives. John was amazed to see our little one in my tummy. I had tears in my eyes. It was amazing. I am an only child, and my parents were happy to see that soon they would be called grandparents. They had even chosen a name for my baby. If it was a boy they would name him Erick. If it was a girl it would be Erica.

After the scan my husband and I went straight for lunch at a luxurious French restaurant in town. In the evening we were invited for dinner at Charles's place. Charles was a friend of my husband. That evening, before we left for Charles's place, I wanted to check my emails. I had one message from Zulu, saying that she would love to go out. I replied that it would be Friday afternoon at Nando's, and I left her my mobile number, just in case she had any problems on the day.

Not a minute later she called me. That meant she must have been online when I replied to her. She was very happy to hear my voice again and I was happy to hear hers, but she said she didn't have much credit and that the line might get cut off. I asked her to hang up and let me call her back. I called her back and off we went:

"Janet, thank you very much for accepting me the way I am. I am very grateful."

"You are welcome. I like you just the way you are."

"Really?"

"Yeah, true."

"Janet, you know what … eh-eh."

"What, Zulu?"

"What is Nando's restaurant like? Is it middle class? Do I have to get my hair done nicely and dress very sexily? Seriously, I have nothing good to look sexy in."

"There you go again, Zulu. You see where your problem is? You don't accept yourself the way you are. Stop comparing yourself to others. Be you and don't try

42

to be someone else."

"But even though I have to be me, I need to be attractive too."

"When you first learn how to be yourself, then you will learn how to be attractive."

"OK. But does that mean I can dress like usual?"

"Yes, that is what I mean and that is what you are supposed to be doing. You work out what you have, and be happy with it. When I read your messages I wasn't very pleased. You just want to work so you can look good and be attractive and not because you want to save your money and perhaps further your education. You told me that you dropped out of school when you were eleven years old. You should be thinking of using the opportunity that your father has given you, by bringing you to this country, to further your education. All the things that you want to have now are only temporary things. Please stop looking at what other people are doing. Look at where you want to be. In short, know what you want and go for it."

"Janet, thank you very much. How much do I need to bring with me to Nando's?"

"No, don't you worry. I will take care of everything."

"Are you sure? I can bring something with me."

"No, don't worry."

"That's kind of you, Janet. Thank you very much."

"You are welcome."

"Thanks. I just don't know why other people don't like me. Most of them see me as an illiterate, but I can be clever and pretty, you know?"

"Good. That's what I want to hear from you. Zulu, you are wise, you are clever and you are pretty."

"Thanks, Janet. You know, it's just that I have come to understand that the success of a person is in the hands of others, because had I been supported through education I would have been studying at university by now. So, you see, I had no support, Janet."

I remained silent for a while on the phone because something had come to mind. I remembered that recently my husband had said something similar to what Zulu had just told me.

"Janet, are you there? Janet …"

"Oh, yes … Yes, I am here. Sorry. I was just thinking of something."

"What is it? Am I not being interesting?"

"No, on the contrary. Actually, you have inspired me with what you just said."

"How?"

"The success of a person is in the hands of others. I am going to write something about this."

"Ha-ha-ha. Something from an illiterate like me."

"Don't start again. Other people may think or speak of you any way they like, but to me you are more than clever."

"Is that just flattery, or do you mean it?"

"I mean it, Zulu. You said something real. In other words, what you said is that people must help one another; countries must get together and help other countries in need, so they too may live a fulfilled life."

"Yes, that is it, Janet. So how are you going to break it down?"

"Don't you worry. I will write something good before we see each other on Friday."

"OK, I will look forward to that. By the way, are you a writer?"

"Not yet."

"I wish you all the best."

"Thanks, love. Oh, my husband is calling me. Got to go now. We are going for dinner at a friend's place. It was nice talking to you again, Zulu. Talk to you tomorrow, OK?"

"Oh, you are married."

"Yes."

"That's very good. OK – run run. Take good care of yourself and of your husband and bon appétit in advance."

"Thanks, Zulu. And be yourself, please."

"It's a promise, Janet."

I felt so comfortable talking to Zulu compared to Naomi. I would rather have gone out to a party with Zulu than with Naomi. Zulu was a source of inspiration for my book. When we came back from Charles's house I didn't sleep all night. I wanted to get something written down about what Zulu had said. As I grabbed a pen and my notebook I could feel myself being inspired and had much to write. I wrote down all that I possibly could on this 'Zulu topic'. I wrote and wrote and when I had finished writing I edited my work, making it not too much but concise and clear to understand. When I had finished editing I was very happy with what I had written, but more importantly I wanted Zulu to see how much she had inspired me.

The next morning Naomi called and asked me to lend her some money. She had to get something but couldn't wait for her wages in two weeks' time. I didn't want to ask her what the money was for; I just asked how much and she said £100.

She explained why she needed the money: "I need to do food shopping, as my fridge is empty. Some friends have been at my place for like a week and they have finished all the food and drinks. Please help me out."

"OK," I said, "I will see what I can do for you, but I cannot promise you an amount. Whatever I get I will surely give it to you."

"Thanks, Janet. What could I have done without you? You are such a darling. God bless you, babe. So when might you be able to give it to me?"

"Just give me like twenty minutes and I will call you back."

"Twenty minutes? That's very long. I am starving."

"Well," I said, "that's the least it will take, but if you leave me now I will see if I can get you something straight away."

She said bye and hung up. I had some savings in my bank account, but the reason why I told her twenty minutes was to think about it first, because I didn't want any trouble in getting my money back from her, since she was a troublemaker. Then I thought, OK, let me just lend her £50. So I rang her back and asked for her bank-account details. I transferred £50 to her account.

As soon as she had cashed the money she rang me back, saying, "I don't know how to thank you. Forever I will be grateful."

"You are welcome," I replied.

She said she would pay me back in two weeks' time.

Friday (4:30pm) at Nando's

Zulu got there on time and was waiting for me outside the restaurant.

"Very punctual and reliable you are, Zulu," I said to her.

She smiled. "Thank you, Janet."

"Shall we go in?"

"Yes, of course."

As we walked into the restaurant we were given seats and then we made our orders. When I asked her what she wanted to order, she said, "Since it's my first time here, let me have the same as you."

Then I saw her taking some money out of her pocket.

"Janet," she said, "I managed to get some money from my father just so I may contribute to the costs of the orders we have made."

I was touched. What a lovely friend she was. To be honest, Zulu was like Stacey, though Stacey was thirteen years older than me and I was one year older than Zulu. Zulu sounded like an old woman in a young lady.

I said, "I am very pleased, Zulu. Thank you very much. But like I said before, I will take care of everything. So keep the money to yourself. Perhaps you might want to get yourself something else."

"Oh, Janet, I insist, please," she said.

I said, "No, Zulu. Buy yourself something you want."

"Well, thanks, Janet. You are very kind. I will take it back to my father, since you don't need it."

Again I was impressed. She would take the money back to her dad – what a good girl she was. Later we were served our food.

"Zulu, are you enjoying your meal?"

"Yes, I am. Thank you."

"Good."

"And you?"

"Yeah, me too."

We both cheered.

While we waited for our desserts, I said, "Zulu, there is something I want to tell you – that is, if you are willing to consider seriously what I am about to tell you. And don't think that I am counselling you, because I am not a counsellor. I am just trying to advise you as a friend. Zulu, you have to bear in mind that you aren't ugly, stupid or whatever people say or think you are. You are pretty, kind, wise and clever. Do you agree with me?"

"Yes, I agree with you, Janet."

"Then you have just signed my agreement, so I will proceed with my speech."

"Ha-ha-ha. What agreement, Janet?"

"Never mind – just being funny. Anyway, like I was saying … So tell me, what are your aims for life, Zulu?"

"Me, eh, I want to further my education. I want to belong to the academic world. This has always been my dream."

"Then why are you driving yourself away from your dream?"

"What do you mean by that, Janet?"

"You want to belong to the academic world, yet you only want to work to buy fancy clothes, accessories and whatever, just so that you may be attractive to people. Is this how you are going to be an academic? Now tell me, what academic person would want to have a friend whose sole concern is her looks, clothes, figure or whatever? To be honest with you, you will only attract those that are also interested in looks, clothes, etc."

"You are very right, Janet, but I can't help it. The humiliation is just too much. I mean, when I go to college for my ESOL (English Speakers of Other Languages) and maths classes every girl is looking good, and me, I am never looking good. I feel so embarrassed, like I want to drown myself in the sea. And my father is always saying, 'I can't give you money now, Zulu. I have bills to pay and so many other things.' I mean, you can just imagine what I am going through."

"Are you happy with what your father tells you?"

"Yes, of course. But it's just that whenever there is a party I am always unwilling to go, because I remember the first time I went to a party I was the only bad-looking lady there, and I felt so embarrassed that I left earlier than expected."

"Let me say this – you are happy with your father, but you are just not being patient enough, because you believe that the competition between young girls nowadays is at a very high level, and you want to keep up to that level."

"Yeah, Janet, that is it! But I am not able to do it. I do get some money from the government, but it's not enough."

"You know, Zulu, it's just a matter of time. Do what you are meant to do for now, which is your English and maths classes, and at the same time try to be doing something good in your free time, something like volunteering to get work experience. Trust me, before you know it you will have achieved something good for yourself and gotten a job. But if you go the opposite way I don't know for how long you can keep looking good when you haven't first of all arranged a fixed income for your life."

"Wow! You are the most intelligent person I have ever met in my entire life!"

"Oh, please don't give me that. I am just advising you as a friend. I hope you will consider all that I have said."

"I will, Janet. What are friends for?"

"Very good. Anyway, one last thing for you – I finally wrote something down about what we discussed the other day."

"Really? Interesting."

"I named the whole thing *Your Success is in the Hands of Others*."

"Wow! Brilliant!"

"I have brought you a copy – it's in my handbag. Do you want to have it?"

"Yes, of course I do! If you must know, I have always been attracted to literature."

"OK, let me get it out for you. And in addition to

this I will be giving you a short story that I wrote a couple of weeks ago. I believe the story is very much related and is a good example of when 'your success is in the hands of others'."

"Thank you so much, Janet. Seriously, I really appreciate this."

"Sure."

"Certain."

"Good. I am happy that you appreciate my help. OK, let's start having our desserts so we can go before my husband gets back from work. I always want him to meet me at home whenever he's coming back from work."

"That is very good. I believe a good wife is always taking good care of her husband, so you are a good wife. Your husband is very lucky to have you. Nowadays young women hardly ever keep the traditional ways of a woman, except for those who are religious."

"Oh, thank you. By the way, do you have a belief?"

"Why do you ask?"

"Because you spoke of religion."

"I have both tradition and religion, but where tradition and religion contradict, religion prevails."

"Interesting. So what religion are you?"

"I belong to the Almighty Lord Jesus Christ."

"You are a Christian."

"Yes I am."

"Same here."

We both laughed.

We left the restaurant around 6 p.m.

Under the title *Your Success is in the Hands of Others*, I wrote:

Your success depends upon the support of others. A child needs parents to take good care of him in order for him to grow. If the child is not well looked after –

that is, if he doesn't eat healthy food or have clean water for drinking or a good environment to live in – this child will live unhealthily and could die very young. Whatever success this child was going to enjoy in life as he grew up will not happen.

Here is another example. My parents were able to take good care of me from the time I was born. They sent me to school, giving me a good education. They wiped my tears every time I cried. They sang songs for me to dance to every time I felt like dancing. They told me stories that I could learn from. They taught me lessons that made me wise and they kept me away from doing wrong. They gave me wings so that I could fly anywhere I wanted to go. They made me smile whenever I was sad and tickled me to make me laugh. They did everything possible to make me happy. If today I am wise and strong, it is because of them. Now, what if I had not been given all this support since birth? Would I have become what I am today? Perhaps I would be dead, or hanging out somewhere on the street.

Every person's success is in the hands of others. If those supporting you are not supporting you sufficiently, it is hard for you to succeed. If you have no support you have no progress.

Here is one final example. Human beings need food and water to survive every day, and these two things have to come from somewhere. We get them from shops or retailers who get the food and water from manufacturers or wholesalers. They in turn get food and water from somewhere. In their case it is from agricultural fields. Now just see the length of the supply chain for all this food and drink. Without the support of agriculture, manufacturers can't get raw materials into finished products. Wholesalers will have nothing to sell, and neither will small shops and retailers. If this happens, people will die of hunger. No one will be able to go to work the next day, so there will be no more business, no more sales, no more pubs, no more clubs, no more elections and, ultimately, no world.

Support breeds success, which is why we need support everywhere we go and in everything we do, be it at home, school, work, in business, in friendship or in love.

The related short story was as follows:

Every person is important

To be important it does not matter who you are or where you come from. Whether you are rich or poor, beautiful or ugly, you are important. Whether you are educated or uneducated, you are important. You are one of the ingredients that make the soup taste good. Without you, the soup would not be as tasty as it is supposed to be. Let me give you an example. One day, a woman collapsed in a little street where few people pass by. The only person present on the street that day was a young girl in her twenties. This girl was not well educated. She did not know how to read, write or speak English. When she saw the woman collapse she ran to the next street for help. The first people she saw were two men. Stopping in front of them, she started to make signs of danger.

The men said, "What is wrong with you? Can you not speak?"

They didn't know that she couldn't speak English. They wanted to leave, but the girl insisted. She continued the signs and finally they understood. The men followed her until they saw where the woman was lying and called an ambulance straight away. At the hospital she was treated and she survived. Now tell me, who was the hero in this case? Who was the key, the direct saviour of the woman's life?

The young girl used her sign language to help save the woman's life. She would not have been seen as important in some situations, but she was certainly important on that day. Without her the woman would have died because no one would have run for help. Can you see how important every person is despite their background? We need each other to communicate. We need each other to help us reach something. We need each other to cooperate in achieving our goals. We should not think of others as idiots just because they have not been to school, nor should we consider people to be important just because they are educated. No one in this world is more important than anyone else. Every person is important.

As soon as I arrived home Zulu texted me, first saying that she was touched by the stories, then asking me to check my emails, saying that she had sent me 'something'. She didn't tell me what it was. When I checked it was two poems that were related to one another. I was very impressed by how creative she was and how she managed to make the English so clear to understand:

We do not say and show everything

I do not need to tell you my plans.
I do not need to tell you my life.
I do not need to tell you my job.
I do not need to tell you that I have a girlfriend.
I do not need to tell you that I have a boyfriend.
I do not need to tell you or show you that I do my homework.
I do not need to tell you or show you that I know

53

how to cook.
I do not need to tell you where I go.
I do not need to tell you or show you what I do.
I do not need to tell you or show you what I have.
I do not need to tell you or show you who I am.

They do not know the truth

They do not know the truth about me.
They do not know the truth about you.
They do not know what is around me.
They do not know what is around you.
They do not know what I am all about.
They do not know what you are all about.
They see my way every day, but they do not know where it goes.
They see your way every day, but they do not know where it goes.
They see me every day, but they do not know who I am.
They see you every day, but they do not know who you are.
We do not care about what they say;
All we know is that we are true.
They criticise us everywhere,
But they do not know the truth.
They do not know what they see,
And it is not everything we say, and show.
So they do not know the truth.

As I read through the two poems I felt inspired to write something back to Zulu regarding this. I got a pen and my notebook, sat on the sofa and started writing. It took me five minutes to write and edit my poem. I couldn't believe that it had only taken five minutes for me to write a short poem when usually it took me about fifteen minutes; this showed how good I was becoming at writing poems and short stories. So I emailed back:

You do not know what you see

You do not know what you see. You think you know but I can tell you that you have no idea. What you see is not what it is all about. The person you see in front of you is not the type of person you think he is. The person you have lived with for years and whom you think you know very well is not the type of person you think he is.

Do not judge others, because you do not know who they truly are.

You do not know what happened to François that made him what he is today.

You never saw Kevin do his homework, so you say that he is lazy and will never pass his exams. You are wrong, because Kevin did his homework at night while you slept.

Do not say that David is wrong, because you do not know what wrong people did to him. You do not know what he is going through.

People do not need to tell you what their plans are; they do not need to tell you what they truly are. Some people keep everything to themselves, so you do not know what you see and therefore you do not have the right to make a judgement.

Then I called Zulu:

"Hey girl, how are you?"

"I am very fine, Janet. Ha-ha, I loved the poem you just sent me. You have said it clearer. What a clever brain you have! Amazing!"

"You are the one who has inspired me again. I loved your two poems and was strongly inspired to write back, so I thought of putting your two poems together

55

and seeing what I could get. I am happy that you have loved the results."

"I have, and I must say you have good writing skills."

"Writing is interesting, trust me."

"Very interesting indeed – you imagine yourself seeing a scene and you try to put it on paper."

"Exactly."

"Janet, I want you one day to achieve your dream of becoming a great writer. Keep on working hard and don't let anyone let you down … Anyway, you already know all **about the angels of the bad side** as you call them, so no need for me to tell you all this again."

"Knowing about something should not stop one from learning further about it, so your advice will always be welcomed."

"You are absolutely right, dear. But some people think when they know about something they know it all, when actually they know nothing at all. And it's not every person who wants to take advice, especially from people like us. So you really are a good person. You accept people the way they are, despite their backgrounds, and I think it's a good thing because God loves us all just the way we are."

"Who are we to choose who to like and who not to like when God himself likes everybody? But if we do choose who to like, that would mean it's not everybody who belongs to God."

"Very true, Janet. And I now see why you talk of **angels of the other side**. Two sides opposite one another. One good side and one bad side; the good side belongs to God."

"And **between** the two sides there is a **street** where we have those people who are still wondering which side to go."

"But they have to stop wondering and make a good

56

decision about which side to go as quickly as possible, because there is no time left."

"And the truth is there has never been time."

"Correct. Janet, there is something you know that I know and that I know that you know."

"All I know is that I will see you there."

"There indeed."

"OK, I won't keep you for long. I have to do something now. You have a great evening and see you hopefully very soon."

"Thanks for calling, dear. See you soon, and my regards to your husband."

"I haven't even talked to him about you yet. I will do that today."

"Take your time. Do it whenever you feel ready."

"Thanks. See you."

"Bye, dear."

I was very surprised to see that Zulu knew what I knew about the **angels of the other side**: the way they stand opposite each other like two buildings with a street between them, with people walking on the street and wondering which building to enter. Fascinating, this was. I wondered how the managers of the bad building kept on attracting customers into their building. I had to know this so that I could see how I would save whatever person they would try to persuade into entering their building. Zulu was possibly an angel of my building, but I had to see to that and with time I surely would.

Some angels of the bad side pretend to be angels of our side just so that they can get to know our secrets of saving people and also to get our angels to learn to do their bad habits. Only at the end do they show their true colours. So it is really hard to tell who is a good or a bad angel, because bad angels also enter our building; we angels of the good side can never tell because you don't know the heart of a man. Only the Lord Jesus can tell. That's the scariest part of it – not knowing who you are talking to or laughing with or who you are letting into your house as a friend. But because He who is above us knows everything there is really no need for us to worry. I mean, what can we do when our powers on earth are limited and we do not know the reason why? The reason is only known to Him who is above us. All we can do is stay in union with Christ.

It is not only Christians who do work within our building, but also those people who are righteous but not religious. I wonder why? It's amazing to see how beautiful our building is and how ugly the opposite one is. But what shocks me the most is that the people on the street do not see how ugly the other building is, both inside and out. Later I would come to understand that they cannot see what I see because they are not standing where I am standing.

The next day my husband and I were to receive guests. Three of my husband's friends were visiting in the evening. That was how I came to meet Tricia.

I cooked some delicious dishes for that special evening. I also made blueberry muffins and chocolate-chip biscuits. I made vanilla ice cream and fruit dessert. Then I thought of inviting my friends, too, so I invited Stacey and her husband. I also asked Zulu to come over. But then I did something perhaps I shouldn't have done and invited Naomi.

My husband's friends were George, Christopher and Charles. Naomi had come with one of her friends, Tricia. I introduced everybody to each other.

Naomi, Tricia and Stacey helped me set the table. Zulu insisted that she help us too so she could learn how to set a table. So five of us set the table, and as we were setting the table Zulu asked me how to eat at the table. Discreetly, so that the others wouldn't hear us, I told her that she should hold the fork in her left hand and the knife in her right hand and be relaxed when picking up her food. When we finished setting the table we called everyone to join us and sit up. We started eating. I was very happy to see how well Zulu managed to eat – she was very quick at learning. Then something happened. As Zulu tried to pick up her glass she accidently poured some juice into Naomi's dish, as she was sitting next to her. I was shocked to see Naomi's reaction.

Naomi: "Look at what you have done. Are you blind or something? My delicious food is spoiled."

Zulu: "I am really sorry, Naomi. I didn't mean for this to happen."

Naomi: "Oh, shut up, you good-for-nothing thing …"

Zulu: "I am not a thing – you know my name."

Naomi: "Who told you that I even want to remember your name? Can't you see what you have done? Don't you have manners at all, or don't you know how to behave when at the table?"

John: "It is OK, Naomi. Let me change your dish for you. As you can see there is still plenty of food on the table, so you can serve yourself again."

Naomi: "Not until I have taught this stupid girl some manners."

Zulu: "Naomi, I have just apologised to you. Please don't embarrass me like this in front of guests. And besides, I am not stupid."

Naomi: "You are so silly. You embarrassed yourself! Don't they teach you manners in Africa?"

Me: "Enough, Naomi! She didn't mean it. Can't you see it was an accident?"

Naomi: "Stop it, Janet! Why are you always coming my way?"

Zulu: "We are taught more than manners in Africa. I believe nobody is perfect and accidents do happen at times. Thank you."

John: "Naomi, she didn't mean it. Could you just say sorry to Zulu for calling her names?"

Naomi: "Sorry for what, John? She's the one who should be saying sorry to me!"

John: "I guess she has said it twice."

Zulu: "Excuse me, dear friends. I just want to go back to the living room. Janet, thanks for the food – it was delicious. John, thanks to you, too."

We were all shocked by Naomi's behaviour. When we had finished eating we all moved into the living room. I went to sit down next to Zulu, just to try to comfort her from the incident. She wasn't really looking unhappy – it was like she had forgotten it all. Naomi and Tricia went to sit next to Christopher, George and Charles. John, Stacey and Paul were looking at something in the garden. Tricia asked George what he did for a living. George answered that he was a solicitor, as were Charles and Christopher. Tricia became eager to make strong contact with George. Making advances towards George she claimed that she was a nurse. "Interesting," said George. She took George's number and invited him to her flat for dinner the next day. As for Naomi, she was first chatting to Charles, but Charles was being very hard with her. Naomi started talking to Charles while Christopher was on his mobile phone with a friend.

Naomi asked Charles, "Are you married?"

"Why do you ask?"

"Nothing, really. Just to know."

"Why do you want to know?"

"Come on, we are all here as friends getting to know each other. I don't see what the big deal is," said Naomi.

"Oh, really ... I guess it's really none of your business," said Charles.

"Anyway, I am a solicitor too," said Naomi.

"I see. And where are your chambers?" asked Charles.

"Oh, I am a trained lawyer."

"So you don't have the LPC, but you are a trained lawyer," laughed Charles. The LPC was the Legal Practice Certificate required by the Law Society for all qualifying solicitors.

"What's that again? LP ... what?" asked Naomi.

"You don't know where your chambers are and you don't know what an LPC is? Can't you see that you are getting confused?" said Charles.

"Oh, you mean where I train," said Naomi.

"Excuse me," said Charles. "I want to go to the toilet."

Not a minute after Charles left for the toilet, and as soon as Christopher got off the phone, Naomi went to sit close to Christopher, with whom she got along quite well. They discussed issue after issue. Naomi changed her story and told Christopher that she was studying for her Master's in Business Administration. I guess Christopher fell in love with Naomi. With her smooth fake voice and sexy body, how could he not have? They got drunk, danced and then decided to both leave early. They were the first pair to leave; then it was Stacey and her husband. An hour later Tricia and George left. So that left me, my husband, Zulu and Charles. Charles told Zulu how sorry he was about Naomi's behaviour but said that she should just let it go, as that was just the way some people were. Zulu was happy to hear this, smiling and saying, "Thank you, Charles."

"You are welcome," he responded.

An hour later Charles left. Half an hour later Zulu decided to leave. I asked my husband if we could drop her off. So we dropped her off. While we were in my husband's car I kept on apologising to Zulu on behalf of Naomi, saying that I was very sorry and she should just forget about Naomi, like Charles said.

"To be honest with you, Janet," she said, "I was not happy at all with the way she spoke to me. I have never been insulted like that before in my life. I am not a child. Even a mother wouldn't speak to her child in such a way for a simple mistake. And she goes telling me about manners – was that a good way of reflecting back to an incident? No, I don't think so. Accidents happen all the time. But it is OK. Not to worry. I am already through with it. She's just another angel of the bad side."

I gave her a big smile because of what she said, and she smiled back.

On our way back home my husband asked me, "What is this thing I am hearing – *'she's just another angel of the bad side'*?"

"Don't you worry, honey. It's a long story," I replied.

I was glad to hear that from Zulu, as it meant that Zulu was beginning to compare the two categories of the 'angels of the other side'. It had become very interesting to see that there were people who were able to see what I could see and understand what I understand.

The next morning Tricia and Naomi came back to my house around 8 a.m. I was still in my pyjamas and was about to have a bath. I was very surprised to see them because of the time and also because they hadn't said that they were coming.

"I guess all is well?" I asked them as I opened the door to let them in.

"Everything is fine," they both responded.

I took them to the living room where I offered them

tea, and toast with butter and fried eggs. I joined them and we ate together. They then told me that their sole reason for coming to see me early that morning was to tell me that I should understand why they had said all those lies to George and Christopher the day before – the reason being that had they told the two men the truth about their jobs (that they worked as cashiers in River Island), the men wouldn't have been attracted to them. But I told them I was not in their game. What if George and Christopher came to find out that they were lying about their occupations? What would be the consequences then?

"Nice house by the way," said Tricia. "I was amazed yesterday to see how beautiful your house is."

"I said that before," said Naomi.

"How old are you, Janet?" said Tricia.

"I am twenty-two years old."

"Twenty two? You've got to be kidding me! And you are married?" said Tricia.

"I said that, too," said Naomi.

"Aren't you too young for marriage?" asked Tricia. "Are you not supposed to be living your life instead of being married to an old man?"

"So Naomi has already told you about my husband? Right."

"Eh-eh," said Tricia. "Not really."

"What do you mean by not really? And by the way, who told you that I am not living my life? Listen, girls, have you just come to my house to find out about my life? How I live my life, know my secrets, pretend to like me? Or have you come to befriend me? Because if you come as spies, trust me – your plans have failed. As you can see, I was about to have my bath and go to the learning centre where I teach. So, sorry – your time is up."

"Not so rude," said Naomi.

"We are just having a girls' talk," said Tricia.

"Well," I said, "your talk is not good for me. So please just leave."

"Oh, babes. What we meant was, have you ever had fun? Like going clubbing?" said Tricia.

"No, Tricia," I replied. "Just stop. It's not going to work. Just leave, please."

"Janet!" shouted Naomi.

"I mean it. Leave my house. Naomi, I have already told you before not to ever call my husband an old man. And you did it to an even greater extent – talking about my husband to Tricia, a girl I don't even know. Listen, I am good to people, even when they try to insult me, but when they keep on causing trouble in my life I show them the door."

"Enough of this crap, Tricia. Let's get the hell out of this old-school mansion," said Naomi.

"It's OK, thank you. Just go and let me and my old-school mansion be."

They left my house singing repeatedly, "Live it up – live your life – that's what we do."

I was so hurt. It was my first time seeing such behaviour. How could one say such words to a fellow friend? Why would anyone want to know so much about your life, like you were a famous pop star? What could be the reasons behind it?

But when I remembered what my father used to tell me, I got the answers to my questions. My father used to say: "It is because they see you shining like a star on the top of the world and want to put out that light that shines on you. They see themselves as inferior to you in some ways and want to minimise you to bring you down to their level."

I refused to talk about it to my husband, because he would just blame me for not listening to him when he said that the girls were no good as friends. I never wanted to see those girls again in my life. But our friendship reconciled somehow, and I lived to regret it.

Two weeks later I was about to go out shopping when I saw an envelope had been posted through my letter box. I opened it and it was written by Naomi. Behind the first letter was another letter which was written by Tricia. The two letters were saying the same thing:

Dear Janet,

We want to apologise for behaving so arrogantly the other day in your house. We know that you might not be from the same class as ours and might not have been brought up in the same way, but please, we meant no harm. We mean this from the bottom of our hearts. We are truly sorry for hurting your feelings. Nobody is perfect. We truly love you though at times we might not show it. Please do not reject or ignore our calls. If we didn't care about you we wouldn't be writing you these letters. Nobody is perfect – I guess we all have our own defects. So please just forgive and forget.

We love you dearly. Please forgive us xxx.

Your dear friends.

I was very angry with myself, because my heart was ready to forgive and forget. What type of heart do I have, I asked myself. I have never been happy with my heart because I am too soft-hearted, and sometimes people take advantage of it, forgetting that I only do what my heart tells me because I want to continue being me and not change myself to something else. This is how God created me to be, and I wouldn't want to be somebody else. My father used to say that people with a good heart have so many blessings and that there is always something great in store for them. So I wouldn't let people change me, as I didn't want to miss out on all the good things that God had kept for me. Therefore, I forgave and forgot about the whole issue. Then I received text messages from the two of them, saying again the same thing: "Thanks for your comprehension." I put the two letters in my bag, came out of the house and locked the door. As soon as I started walking down my street to go and get my bus to the city centre, two voices behind me whispered, "Hello Janet."

It was Tricia and Naomi.

"You guys scared me," I said. "Please don't do that again."

"Oh, sorry. We just wanted to surprise you," said Tricia.

"Don't tell me that you were hiding somewhere near my house, waiting for me to come out?"

"Oh yes we were, darling," responded Naomi.

"You guys have nothing to do instead?" I asked. "Like work or college?"

"We are off work today, so we decided to come and wait for you outside so we could personally say sorry," said Naomi.

"But we had no agreement to meet today. And what if I hadn't come out today?"

"We would have had no choice but to come and ring your doorbell," said Tricia.

"And what if I didn't open?"

"Then we would have waited until you opened the door," said Tricia.

"You two are very funny. Anyway, I have forgiven you guys, but on the condition that you don't repeat what you did."

"Oh, thank you, love," they both shouted.

"Please keep your voices down. We are in a quiet neighbourhood."

"Whatever – we are just happy that you have forgiven us. Thank you so much, Janet," said Tricia.

"Yeah, Janet. We are truly thankful," said Naomi.

"It's OK. So now where are you guys going to?"

"Nowhere, actually. And you?" said Tricia.

"I want to get some new flowers at the florist for my garden."

"We can accompany you, if you don't mind," said Tricia.

"OK. If you say so. Thank you."

So that was how we were reconciled. They came with me to the florist and even helped me carry my flowers home. We had lunch together, and then they helped me plant the new flowers in my garden. They even helped me cook dinner for me and my husband. They left my home around 5 p.m. – just an hour away from the time my husband was due home. I was so touched by the way they had changed all of a sudden and were trying to be good to me – but it was not the first time for Naomi to have done so, and I didn't yet know Tricia, so I still wanted to be careful with them. There was no way for me to trust them again just as easily as that. I decided to continue observing them and keep the friendship at a limit which I believed would not cause me any trouble.

Two days later Tricia visited me again and brought me some red apples and melons. We made blueberry muffins and chocolate-chip biscuits and watched movies. We spent the whole day together, and she only left when my husband came home.

One day in October I called Naomi and asked her about my £50. It had been two months since I lent her the money. She had not said anything about it since, and she told me that she had given the money to Tricia. I called Tricia, but Tricia said Naomi hadn't given her any money to give to me. I called Naomi again. She wouldn't answer my calls, so I texted her a message saying that I wasn't her fool and that she should not try to play me.

I forgot about the £50 in question because I didn't want my husband to find out about it. Naomi had just made a fool of herself, because there was no way I would ever lend her any amount of money again.

Chapter 4

It was 21 November: Tricia's birthday. George, her fiancé (who was also my husband's friend), had booked a very nice hall for her birthday celebration. The hall was beautifully decorated and the party well organised. George had invited big people for this special event and Tricia had invited all of us. I didn't want to go because of what my husband had told me about Tricia, and also I had lately been feeling very tired. I was six months pregnant. But Zulu forced me to go as she was dying to go to a party.

Before we left for the venue we were all getting dressed at my place: me, Naomi, Zulu and Tricia. It was fascinating to see how jealous Naomi could be in such situations. Naomi swore that she would have her own birthday party too, when the time came. Naomi had come with three sexy party dresses and asked us to vote on which one she would wear. We all picked the short pink dress. I was wearing a light-blue short-sleeved shiny long dress. Zulu was wearing some black trousers and a black top. To Naomi, what Zulu was wearing wasn't a party outfit. For the very first time I saw Naomi being nice to Zulu. She said that Zulu could choose one of her dresses.

Zulu looked at me and hesitated.

"Go on, Zulu," I said, "pick a dress of your choice."

She picked the short black dress. Zulu couldn't believe that it was the same Naomi being nice to her. "Thank you very much, Naomi. I am truly grateful."

"It is OK," responded Naomi.

"Well, girls," said Tricia, "it's my turn to put on my dress. And believe me when I tell you that you all will fall in love with it. My man George bought it for me

69

especially for my birthday. Isn't that so sweet?"

"Sweet, whatever," said Naomi. "It is the first time your man is buying you something. My man does that all the time."

"Oh, hell no – it's not the first time," said Tricia. "It's just that this one is not any dress. It's Rebecca Taylor. Have you heard of it?"

"What the hell … Who doesn't know the Rebecca Taylor brand? You should be telling Zulu and not me. Just put the dress on and let's see, instead of talking shit," said Naomi.

"And why Zulu, if I should ask you, Naomi?" I said.

"Well … because she's the one coming from Africa, and they wouldn't have such brands there, would they?" answered Naomi.

"Well, that's not a fair thing to say, Naomi. You shouldn't be making reference to something else when the question was directly addressed at you," I told her.

"Janet, please," she replied. "Could we just stop right now? Because I don't want to go crazy and then have all you people start saying *Naomi has done this, Naomi has done that*. I would rather save my energy for the party than stand here and answer your stupid questions!"

"When will you ever accept that you are wrong?" I continued.

"Janet, it is OK," said Zulu.

"No, it is not OK, Zulu," I said.

"Hey, girls, cut it out, please," said Tricia. "I am the one who started all this up. Can we just forget it all and let me put on my dress?"

We were all amazed by how beautiful the dress was. The style and design of the dress was stunning.

"It must have cost him a fortune," said Zulu.

"Trust me, Zulu – when it comes to me, my man would buy me anything I want," responded Tricia.

"Well, just don't make the guy go bankrupt," said Zulu with a smile.

Tricia laughed.

Naomi became very silent as she stared at Tricia's sexy short-sleeved long red dress. "Anyway, I need to call my new guy Spencer to see if he's already on his way to the party."

"You mean you haven't invited your boyfriend, Kevin?" said Tricia.

"That cheat? Anyway, I have invited him, too, but I also wanted Spencer to be there," responded Naomi.

"Come on, Naomi. Why would you do a thing like that? How can you invite your boyfriend and at the same time invite a guy you know you fancy a lot?" said Tricia.

"Well, the answer to your question is I want to show Kevin that he's not the only cute-looking guy in the whole wide world. That I have a handsome bunny cuter than he is," said Naomi.

"I am not happy with your idea, Naomi," Tricia replied. "There are some decent friends of George who are also attending the party, so please don't make your two guys fight at my party. You know yourself how crazy Kevin can go."

"Not to worry, babe. I know what I am doing. I have everything under control," said Naomi.

It was George himself who came to pick us up. My husband refused to attend the party, as he was not in favour of the idea of George organising a party for Tricia, a lady who kept on taking from George's wallet like a gold-digger. My husband was worried about his friend George. My husband told me that Tricia once asked George, in front of him, to buy her a pair of Versace shoes that cost £800, saying that if he didn't buy them she was not going to make love to him. When my husband said that he thought that was a lot of

71

money to spend on a pair of shoes, Tricia replied with, "John, is it your money? What is your problem? Just zip it and watch me!"

My husband then backed down and said, "Oh no, it's not. You are absolutely right. Excuse my manners."

John was disappointed in George and wondered how a man of such great character and responsibility could stoop so low to a woman like Tricia. But there was nothing he could do, as it was none of his business. My husband also said that George once told him that the sole reason why he would never refuse Tricia a thing was that he had never before had a sexy woman like Tricia who knew how to give it to him in bed. I guess Tricia knew how to work George out. They really had a good scheme going, her and Naomi, and I never came to find out what that scheme was.

The party was brilliant and everybody was enjoying it. Then some other news came up. George proposed to Tricia in front of the crowd. It was amazing not to me but to others who did not know. I was worried instead. Worried that Tricia only loved George because of his money. But, again, who was I to judge? So I let things be.

There really was a good mood at the party. Kevin – Naomi's boyfriend – had joined the party and brought with him some funny funky dances. Naomi and Kevin danced together. They were both very funny to watch as they were always quarrelling, but they made a good couple.

A nice butter cream cake coloured in white, pink and red was later cut, which we all enjoyed. Then another thing came up. Tricia and Naomi were taking pictures of themselves all over the place. They asked me and Zulu to join them. When we had all finished taking pictures, Naomi said, "I can't wait to put my pictures on Facebook."

"Me too," said Tricia.

"Facebook … What is Facebook?" asked Zulu.

Naomi and Tricia laughed.

"You don't know what Facebook is?" said Naomi.

"What is funny here, girls? I wouldn't be asking you if I knew," said Zulu.

"Never mind," said Tricia. "Facebook is a social networking website where you can share pictures with friends and family and exchange messages. Friends and family can like or comment on your photos. But before then you have to register and create your personal profile and then add some friends," said Tricia.

"Oh really? So could you help me open one?" asked Zulu.

"Yes, of course," replied Naomi. "If you come to our place tonight, when we post our pictures we will help you register and create your personal profile," said Naomi.

"Oh, that's so great, girls. But I won't be able to come with you tonight. As you can see, it's already late. By the way, do you and Naomi live together?"

"Yeah, we share the same house, but each with our own bedroom. You could sleep over and go home tomorrow if you want?" said Tricia.

"No, I can't do that," said Zulu. "My father won't let me anyway. I would prefer to come tomorrow," said Zulu.

"OK, suit yourself," said Tricia.

"Tricia, eh-eh, but before then can I have your number so I can call you tomorrow and get directions to your house?"

"Sure," responded Tricia.

That was how Tricia and Zulu exchanged numbers. Zulu then rushed to me, asking me if I also had a Facebook account. I told her that I had heard about it but didn't have one. She was very surprised that I didn't have one. As we were all talking about Facebook some handsome-looking guy walked into the party. He blew everybody away with his beautiful blue-green eyes. No girl could take their eyes off him. When I took another close look at him I realised that I had seen him before somewhere and I remembered that it was Naomi's friend Spencer. Naomi left Kevin and walked towards Spencer, gave him a kiss on his lips and offered him a place to sit down just next to where we were all sitting. She offered him food and some wine. Were they going out together, I wondered? Naomi confused me at times; one minute she wanted Kevin, the next minute Spencer, then Christopher … I kept in mind that she wanted to get back at Kevin, as she had said herself earlier on. But her behaviour towards Spencer at Stacey's birthday party showed that she was madly in love with Spencer. Anyway, it was none of my business.

The next thing I saw was Kevin walking towards Naomi and Spencer.

Kevin went crazy. "What's the fucking meaning of this, Na?"

Naomi remained silent.

"I am talking to you, Na," Kevin went on. "Don't pretend you haven't seen me standing here in front of you!"

Naomi still remained silent.

Kevin shouted, "Naomi, I am talking to you! Who is this fucking guy I am seeing you with? Answer me, Na!"

"Oh yeah? You really want to know? He's some guy I love and really want to be with!"

"Is this some kind of a joke, or … Wait a minute. Are you trying to get back at me or what?"

"Hell yeah! I am getting my revenge on you. You think I feel good when I see you all the time with some girls … sleeping around?"

"So this is a way to get back at me … Bitch."

"If I am a BITCH then you are a CHEATER!"

"Are you better yourself? You are no good anyway. You have just made things easier for me, Na. This relationship is over! Over! And I mean it!"

"Then so be it, you son of a whore! Get out of this party now!"

"Don't you worry, I will be going girl. But before I go, let me just tell you that you were nothing to me but a simple friend. Whenever my good girls were not around, that was the only time I brought you along. So see you really meant nothing to me."

"Get out!" she sobbed. "Go away!"

"I am going. I am going."

Then Spencer said to Kevin, "Hey man, wait a minute. How can you embarrass your girl like this in front of people? She's hurt, man."

"Do you mean your girl? Because as far as I am concerned," said Kevin, "I don't see my girl anywhere around at this party."

"Listen, man, we are just friends and nothing else. Come on, give the girl some respect. You know how jealous girls can be when they find out that their guy is sneaking around with some girls and want to get them back. So forgive her. As you can see, we are not dating. We last met at my friend Stacey's party, and after that we became friends. So cool down man and go get your girl. Just apologise to her."

"If you say so, bro," said Kevin.

"I mean it, man. Go and get your girl. You are the man," said Spencer.

"Thanks, bro. No, you are the man." Kevin laughed.

Kevin went back to Naomi. He apologised to her.

"Did you really mean what you said when you said I mean nothing to you and called me a bitch?" asked

Naomi.

"Come on, Na, I didn't mean it. I was only angry seeing you with another man."

"Swear that you didn't mean it," said Naomi.

"I swear, man! What's wrong with you, Na? I didn't mean it!" shouted Kevin.

They continued doing their thing while Spencer went and sat next to Zulu and they started talking. I felt like Zulu was uncomfortable talking to him, perhaps because I was also sitting next to them, so I excused myself and went to sit next to Tricia and George so that I couldn't hear the conversation between Zulu and Spencer.

A few hours later I became worried about the time. It was 11 p.m. I asked Zulu if we could leave because it was getting late. She was OK to leave. Spencer gave her a peck. Zulu went crazy and couldn't even find her way to the door we had come in by. She was panicking. We didn't bother asking George to give us a lift back because we were going to different destinations and I didn't see how he would have been able to give us a lift given that Tricia had got her hands all over him. We called a cab instead.

At home I had a bath. When I walked into the bedroom I saw my husband fast asleep. I didn't want to make any noise as I didn't want to wake him up.

As I eased myself into bed a voice said, "So how was it?"

"Gosh honey," I said, "I thought you were sleeping."

"How can I sleep when my woman is still out late at night?"

"Come on, honey, you know it was a party. I have never stayed out till this time before. Have I? I was just trying to have some fun."

"It's just that I am beginning to think about these new friends of yours. After the incident that happened between Naomi and Zulu the other day I am beginning to worry about how this relationship between you girls will end."

"How it will end? What do you mean?"

"Your friends are not good friends – I mean Tricia and Naomi. I don't like them."

"Come on, honey, nobody is perfect. Sometimes you just have to take people the way they are."

"But not anybody and particularly not these two ladies. They are talkative, bold for nothing, disrespectful … In fact, they are not good friends, and what I want from you is to stop seeing them."

"I have told you, I just wanted to please Zulu."

"You don't let friends make you do something you don't want to do simply because you want to please them."

"OK. I won't do it again. I mean, personally, I don't want to be their friend, but it's just that they keep coming to me and I don't know what to do."

"Next time, if they ask you to do something for them or go somewhere with them tell them that you are busy. Simple."

"Alright. But honestly I am very sorry for staying out late."

"It's OK. So how was it?"

"Well, the venue was amazing. Tricia was looking very pretty and sexy. George was looking cute in his red suit. There were a lot of people …"

"Red suit? George in red? That's weird. I have never seen him in red before."

"With a green tie."

"A green tie? Ha-ha-ha. Red and green? No way."

"I am serious! And he proposed to Tricia."

"So soon? That Tricia has really taken hold of his mind."

"I thought as much."

"But I am happy for him, as long as he's happy."

"True, I am happy for them too. So how much did you miss me?"

"I missed you so much, but I want you now more than ever!"

The following evening Zulu called me to tell me that she'd been at Tricia and Naomi's place earlier in the afternoon and they had helped her register with Facebook. She wanted to come to my house the next day so that I could help her take some pictures for her to put on her Facebook profile, as she didn't yet have any pictures. The girls said that they didn't want to give her the pictures they'd taken at the party because her face did not look pretty in them. I asked her why she wanted to take pictures at my place when her father or sisters could do that for her. She said it was because my house was nice, especially the garden, and would give her pictures a very good background. So I said it was OK.

She came the next afternoon. We spent the whole day together. I took some beautiful pictures of her in the garden and the living room. I loved her pictures, they were really nice. She posted her pictures and waited for somebody to like or comment on them. She was so impatient. She just wanted somebody to like or say something about her pictures, but nobody did. I told her to have more patience: maybe they hadn't been seen yet by anybody. Then she decided that we should write some poems while we waited. She said that she wanted to write about how she felt back in Africa when things were really hard for her. So she wrote the following:

My present worries me and my future scares me

78

There is someone fighting so hard for a life that could take his existence away. A hand is working so hard, but working without fixed recompense. A foot is finding it hard to move; all movements are blocked by two big opponents.

He is in the middle of two major opponents. In front of him a huge fire is burning, while behind him is a great ocean. To get where he wants to go he must cross the fire, which would burn him to death. If he decides to move back he must try to swim the ocean, but he would surely drown.

He stands there, hoping for firemen to come or for a boat to take him elsewhere. Without this, the fire would burn him or the waves would take him away. Can he survive?

Can he walk the fire without getting burned or swim the ocean without drowning? How long should he wait for the firemen or a boat? Can his guardian angel get him out of the situation?

He is still there, confused and worried about his present and scared of his future; he does not know what to do.

"What is the pain behind this poem?" I asked Zulu.

"There is so much pain to tell, Janet," she replied, "but I guess I will never get to say it all. Only questions remain. Why is the world not equal? Why do some people have to suffer and others not? Why can't we all be happy at once? Or could it be that there is no love in this world? I would really like to get answers to these questions before I leave this world. In Africa things are very different from the way they are in Europe. There is too much suffering there, more than there is here. Do you know why?"

"To be honest with you, Zulu, I don't know the answers to your questions. But there is something I know. Before I tell you what I know that could be a clue to your answers, I firstly want you to know that there is what I call **'causing something'**, which is very different from **'allowing something'**. And there is also what I call **'changing someone's state of mind'**. So an example of a country causing the suffering of its people would be where a government or the state does not spend its money or resources on the poor but instead spends it on themselves and their families by buying their own properties and going on luxurious holidays, etc. Or where the state in question has received some money from another state to help its poor people, but the leaders choose to spend the money on themselves rather than on the poor. Based on this, this particular state is causing the suffering of its people by not putting the money or resources where they are supposed to put them – that is, helping the poor. Whereas allowing something is where a state recklessly allows another state to use its resources, leaving it with very little or nothing for its own people. Here the state has allowed itself to be manipulated, and therefore they have allowed the suffering of their people.

"Now coming to *changing someone's state of mind*, I call this a mental injury, because this is where a person influences another person's mind in a negative way, causing him an injury to the mind that changes the original state of his mind so that he no longer thinks or does what he usually does or wants to do, but instead does something else or something bad to himself or others. This could be applied to any individual, but because we are talking in the context of governments I will stay on the subject. So a president of a particular government may be a good-hearted person and want to help his people to the fullest, but the people around him could fill his mind with bad ideology which would then change his state of mind and make him do an act he wouldn't otherwise have done. For example, a rich man tries to give bread to a poor man, and another rich man comes out and says to the rich man, 'Don't give this poor man bread – he will be the first to come and rob your home!' By saying this, the second rich man has negatively influenced the first into not giving his bread to the poor man. But then everything relies upon the person who is being influenced, because you can either accept the influence or reject it.

"Secondly, this is a world where the good and the bad both exist. Good people are working hard to save people and at the same time bad people are working hard to destroy people. In governments there are also good and bad people. So if a country has a good government, that country might perhaps have less suffering. Having said that, I also want you to know the position of the citizens of a given state. Citizens of a particular state enter into a **social contract** with the state whereby they give their freedom to the people in power in exchange for what I call **life commodities** such as money, education, work, health services, justice, and so on. The state makes a set of rules or laws which the citizens are bound to respect/comply with, and if a citizen is in breach of any of the rules there is a penalty – in some countries all of the life commodities are taken away from the citizen. But if you were to ask me whether there is **law or justice** in this world? In my opinion I would say no, there isn't. There is no law in the world, because the word 'law' is too perfect in itself to be practised in the way it's being practised. There have been many miscarriages of justice. Judges bring ideology into the law when they interpret the law, resulting in judges themselves making their own laws. For me the first innocent person that died on earth made the law void because the law shouldn't have had a single miscarriage. That is why it is called 'law' – it is

fairness and so perfect in itself. The law for me became a policy, a policy that is still in place in order to keep order in a society. The oddest thing about this policy is that this policy is a system. The system cannot die for us; we have to die for the system. Whether you are guilty or innocent when accused of breaching a rule of law, you must pay for it. We all die for this system at one point or another in order to get the system going. For example, here in the UK, be it in criminal cases or others, if you have a good lawyer, whether you are innocent or guilty, you are likely to win the case, because the party with the strongest legal representative or with the strongest evidence wins the case. Now the painful part of this is where a guilty person wins the case and the innocent person pays the price – what a miscarriage of justice this is. So, for me, this is how the system works: we die for the system. Juries could never stop giving out their sentences simply because one or two miscarriages have taken place in the judicial system, but we the citizens have to continue giving our freedoms to the system because that is what the social contract we entered into is all about. The system will die when the world ends."

After I had finished my explanation Zulu became very silent. Then she said, "Janet, oh my God … How did you come about all this? You are right, you know. In Africa, especially, poor children work hard, sleep in bad conditions, and have no good water to drink and no healthy food to eat. In fact they live a life of misery incomparable to those other African children whose parents are involved in government posts. How can we explain this? In Africa the poor have entered into a social contract where they have given their freedom to the government in exchange for nothing. And I mean nothing! Janet, take this poem I have just written now. Read it and you will come to understand the life of the

poor in Africa."
All lights are off

There are assassins among us who are willing to drive us all to hell.
They force us to do what we don't want to do and think it is all well.
They have killed many of us but it's like they are willing to kill the rest.
We know that this is wrong but there is no way we can protest.
They say they will harm anybody who dares to manifest.
They have put us in the darkness and let themselves in the light. This is so unfair.
Because I was told that where there is love all is fair.
And that justice was never unfair.
We sit in the dark alone without them and without knowing their intentions towards us. Because the lights are off we are unable to know what's in the future for us.
There is nothing left for us, no hope, nothing, so I cannot say 'I must'.
But why does it have to be us?
All we can see is the difference in the eyes of the different people that we are.
They have drawn something called a barrier so that we don't get along with them,
But this is wrong says my mother.
Why not love one another?
As I sit in my corner I can hear people crying.
Children crying and dying,
But there is nothing I can do.
We need light to survive.
I sit there in my corner, scared of what will happen to me tomorrow.

I pray to God to send someone to turn on the lights that have been off for centuries, setting us free.

There are tears in my eyes. For one more time I cry to God that if I die tomorrow, may He take my body and place it in His house where the lights are never off and where I always wished to live.

I had tears in my eyes after reading this. People go through a lot all around the world. There are so many untold stories in this world. I laugh while others cry. I eat while others starve to death. How can we complain about our lives when there are people who have never had a life? Think about this deeply when you go to bed. Just imagine exchanging your life with that of others around the world. Try and be them for a while, and trust me you will keep smiling for the rest of your life, thanking God that at least you have a life.

"Janet!" said Zulu. "Janet! Some people have liked my pictures. Janet … Are you OK?"

"Oh yes, I am OK. I was just thinking of something." I quickly wiped away my tears.

Zulu was worried. "What is it, Janet?"

"Nothing, really. You were saying something."

"Oh yes. Naomi, Tricia and Spencer have liked my pictures and album."

Zulu was very happy that her pictures had been liked. I was happy for her too.

"That's very good. I hope this has put a smile on your face."

"Yes, it has. And Spencer left a comment saying, 'You are beautiful.' Oh my God, Janet, I am so happy."

"Is it the same Spencer who is a friend of Naomi?"

"Yes, it's him. I almost forgot to tell you that he said to me the other day at Tricia's birthday party that he likes me so much."

"Really? And you believed him?"

84

"I did. Why not?"

"Just be careful. You never know. And I don't want you to get hurt or be in trouble with Naomi."

"Naomi again, why?"

"The guy is so handsome and Naomi only likes cute guys like him. She told me herself how much she likes the guy. Didn't you hear her say something like that the other day when we were dressing up at my place?"

"Oh yeah. But trust me, I won't let her come my way again, not this time. I once lost love in my life, and I won't lose it twice. Trust me, Janet, I won't let it happen this time."

"Sorry about that, but just watch your back."

"Thank you."

"You are welcome. Zulu, eh-eh, do you mind if we take a walk to the local park? I feel like walking."

"Sure, why not."

We had to put some very warm clothes on as it was quite cold outside. We took with us some sandwiches and hot drinks. We played games together, like hide and seek. We were running all around the park like children. It was amazing. Every time Zulu was around me I felt joy and peace. No arrogance, no bullying and no insults. She was just so amazing. Then we went to sit on a bench. She said that I should come up with another game.

"OK," I said, "I will come up with a game where we don't have to be running around. Let's vote on how handsome any guy that passes by is."

"Now, where is that coming from?" she asked.

"Naomi taught me," I replied.

Zulu agreed to play. The first guy that passed by I gave 5/10 and she gave 8/10. I gave the second guy 9/10 and she gave him 2/10. We both laughed. Then we changed to something else. We decided to tell each other tales.

I asked her to start first. "Zulu, you have some lovely tales in Africa. I found out about this on the CBeebies TV channel where they show *Tinga Tinga Tales* from Africa."

"You've got to be kidding me, Janet – you watch a children's channel? You are such a baby." She laughed.

"Trust me, I do. I like watching anything that's good and moral." I laughed with her.

"I see. So you want a tale from Africa."

"Yes, I do, dear friend."

"Alright, the story I am going to tell you now is a very funny one. The title is *Misunderstanding and Bad Communication Kills*.

"In the 1930s, in the little village of NgaNga Lingolo, south of Congo Brazzaville, lived three friends and their wives. They shared a compound where each couple had a little flat.

"When Brazzaville was colonised by the French, Brazzavillois started giving French names to their children; this happened all over the nation. These three friends were among those people to whom their parents had given French names.

"The three, Pierre, Jean and Luka, were among the first to attend school, but whether they were really attending school or not remains a question.

"One day, the village was given an educator, a new chief who came from the city of Brazzaville. He only spoke French and did not speak Lari, a local village language which is mostly spoken in the south of the country, with any fluency. Should the chief have taken an interpreter with him? Who knows? It was difficult to find an interpreter in those days. The chief's name was Gibier a Poil, which means 'Ground Game' in English. He came straight from the city and his aim was to help the villagers of NgaNga Lingolo learn about Western civilisation.

"Before Ground Game arrived, the ancient chief told the villagers that they should obey the new chief and do exactly as he said.

"When Ground Game first arrived in the village he chaired a meeting to present himself to the villagers and also so that he could get to know them.

"As the meeting started, the chief said in French, 'Bonjour à tous,' which means 'Good morning everybody'. But what the villagers heard, in their native Lari, was *Bon na Tou* – the names of two villagers. The villagers then started shouting at Bon and Tou, telling them that the chief had called them to the front. Bon and Tou went to the front, but the chief did not understand why. He thought that these two men were just excited to see him. So he continued, saying 'Quel monde!', which means 'What a crowd!' But the villagers heard, in Lari, *mangua*, which means 'mango', so they went to get mangos. Then the chief noticed that all the villagers had gone. He wondered what had happened and started to get worried. Then he saw the crowd coming back from the mountains around the village with mangos. For a second time he did not understand.

"When the villagers arrived back with their mangos the chief was very angry and said 'Êtes-vous fou?', which means 'Are you crazy?' But the villagers heard *foufou* – a sort of semolina which was a basic commodity that the whole Brazzaville population ate. The villagers went home to make foufou, which they brought back to the chief. This time the chief understood that something was wrong with his accent or his communication. With the little Lari he knew he asked the villagers if there were people who could speak and understand French. The villagers responded that there were some people who went to school and might be able to interpret. These three were Pierre, Jean and Luka. The three friends came to the chief as interpreters. The chief decided to call them one at a time, starting with Pierre, to whom he said, 'Pierre, dit au villageois qu'ils doivent commencer à porter des jeans.' This means, 'Pierre, say to the villagers that they should start wearing jeans.' Pierre told the villagers that they should wear their friend Jean. The villagers tried to remove Jean's clothes, but the chief stopped them and blamed Pierre, saying that he'd lied about being able to interpret, when plainly he could not. Pierre responded that he was only a French interpreter: the word 'jean' that he knew was the name Jean, while the other 'jean' with an added 's' was an English word. The chief asked him to leave the meeting immediately, so Pierre went home to his wife.

"The chief then called Jean, the victim of the first attempt at interpretation. He said to Jean, 'Nous allons maintenant joué à un jeu de pierre pour vous faire oublier le malentendu qui vient de se produire,' which means, 'We are now going to play a stone game to help you forget the misunderstanding that has just taken place.' The stone game was played by the Brazzavillois. It involved digging about twelve holes and putting three small stones in each. It was played by regrouping all the stones into one hole by passing each and every stone into a hole without leaving a stone in any of the other holes. Jean said to the villagers, 'The chief has said that you should now go and play Pierre.' The villagers went to Pierre's home, took him and started playing with him, bouncing him up and down. Pierre managed to escape, but was quite badly hurt and ran back home to his wife.

"When the chief saw what had happened to Pierre he told Jean to leave. He then looked for Luka, but he had run away because of the brutality that had happened to his friends.

"The chief could find no one else to hire as an interpreter and so decided to do as he had been doing at the beginning of the meeting. He shouted to the crowd in French, 'Cherchez-moi Luka!', or 'Find Luka for me!' The villagers heard *Luka*, which means 'vomit' in Lari. The villagers began to put their fingers into their mouths to make themselves vomit. In pain as they pushed their fingers deep into their mouths, they started to cry, complaining that God had sent a monster to them. As they cried, Pierre's wife arrived, still angry at the beating of her husband. She shouted in Lari to the chief, 'Oh, Ground Game, what have you done to my husband?' The villagers heard this and said, 'Yes, this chief is a ground game because he is different from us, and since he has arrived he has been causing nothing but trouble.' They stopped vomiting and sent him out of the village. The chief went back to the city and the villagers felt freed from everything. Each of them went home in peace."

"What a wonderful story that was, Zulu! I knew you people had wonderful tales there. I absolutely loved it. Please can I have another one?"

"Janet, it's supposed to be your turn now, isn't it?"

"I know, but just one more before I tell you mine. Please."

"OK – one last one. Now this one is called *I Have Lived among Them and Believe Me They Have Nothing Good*, and it's very funny too. Don't mind the tale, it's just for comedy. We tell it all the time to give ourselves a laugh. I lived among them. OK, here we go.

"I lived with people who walked with one foot. As they walked with one foot I did the same, but it did not make any sense. What was the other foot doing? They were not going very far as they walked like chameleons and would spend years to get to their destinations.

"I lived with liars and jealous people and found that

they have nothing good; they do not progress. They spend time telling lies about others just because they find themselves inferior to them. It is stupid. Why don't they work at making themselves superior, instead of recycling their own lies?

"I lived with the rich and they have nothing good. Money has not brought them all the happiness they wished for.

"I lived with criminals and they have nothing good. They commit crimes, forgetting that one day they will be arrested.

"I lived with Mrs Mistake and she has nothing good. She has made many mistakes without learning from them and has just made another one.

"I lived with Miss Talkative and she has nothing good. She spends time talking with friends, forgetting she has left a pot on the fire.

"I lived with politicians and believe me they have nothing good. They set good pretexts but the public ends up discovering the truth.

"I lived with receivers and they have nothing good. They receive goods, gifts, cheques and love, but they are never grateful to their givers.

"I went out with the law one day and believe me the law has something wrong. The law found all guilty, but failed to bring about true justice even half of the time.

"I lived with the poor and they have nothing good. Instead of thinking about what they are going to eat tomorrow, they only think of overcoming those who mock them.

"I lived with warriors and believe me they have nothing good. They have lost the battle and have been disarmed, yet they want to declare another war.

"I lived with Sir Heart. Sir Heart has only one heart and only one place within that heart, yet he wants to love a second woman. Where will he place her?"

I laughed. "Very funny."

"Very funny, isn't it?"

"But seriously Zulu, it is very funny. Ha-ha-ha! Did you make it up yourself?"

"This one? No, I didn't. I was told it by my grandmother. I made the first one up myself back in primary school. OK, enough with the laughing. You tell me your story now."

"Gosh, you made the first one up yourself? Zulu, you are so clever!"

"Thank you, Janet. Well, like I have always said, I never had the support to develop my educational skills, which is a shame. Every person I told the tale to at the time was amazed to see that a ten-year-old like me could write such an interesting story. And I still have the notebook where I wrote it; I brought it with me. I couldn't have left it back home because this story is my life. It came from my brain and it will live in me forever."

"You are amazing, Zulu. And trust me, you now have the opportunity to fulfil your dream in this country, don't you worry ... Gosh, you write too ... And could you be from the Republic of Congo?"

"Yes, I do write, Janet. I received a little education in primary school, and when I stopped going to school I decided to spend my time reading and writing about this wicked world."

"But you must have a brain, Zulu, girl. You must be so clever to be able to make up stories like this. And where is the Republic of Congo? Are you from that place?"

"Yes I am, Janet. I know I have never told you about where I come from. Republic of Congo, also known as Congo Brazzaville, is situated in the centre of Africa, next to the Democratic Republic of Congo, Gabon, Angola and Cameroon, etc. I am Congolese, Janet.

Now you know."

"I will have to do some online research about your country to find out more. I am already in love with it."

"Janet, I am still waiting for my story."

I laughed. "OK, let me tell you mine. My story is called *The Solution Road.*

"It was 9 p.m., the end of the day. It was time for me to go to bed. As I threw myself into bed I fell asleep immediately. Suddenly, in my dream, I found myself somewhere very dark with no one around and I was scared. I looked around; no one was there and I saw only a big signpost which carried the words *The Solution Road.* Before I decided to walk down the road, I looked at myself and said, 'I think it is time for me to end all the problems that have been disturbing me through my life. My misery will end today, my pains and sorrows will go away, my tears will be wiped dry and I will live happily for the rest of my life.' After saying this I walked down the road. It was a long way, but I continued walking. For a very long time I walked, until I arrived at Solution Road. I could not believe the size of the crowd that I saw. What a crowd it was; I had thought I would be the only one there. I had not been expecting people at such a hidden and mysterious place. I started to ask each person what they were doing there, and they all told me that they had come for a solution to their problems. I asked the nature of their problems and each of them told me. I felt ashamed of myself because their problems were so much worse than mine. Their lives were utterly miserable. Their pains and sorrows were enormous compared with mine. I started thinking, saying to myself, 'Oh my God, I am the only one with such small problems, yet I dare to think I am the person with the worst difficulties in the world. I am much better off than any of these people.' As I was thinking, a bright light seemed to come out from nowhere, while a disembodied male voice spoke from the light. The voice asked what we were all doing there. The crowd answered that they were there to solve their problems. The voice asked the crowd to explain their problems, which they did. I felt ashamed because my problems were too insignificant for the crowd and the problem solver to hear, so I decided to make my weary way home. I left the crowd and walked the same route back, until I got home.

"The next morning when I woke up, the first thing I said was, 'Let it be.' The end."

Zulu became very silent. She didn't respond to my story, so I said, "Zulu, you said nothing about my story."

"Janet, this story is directed at me. It's so related to me. When did you write it?"

"A couple of months ago. I think in May. Why?"

"Janet, I am not the only person who has lost it all. I have to let things be. I am not the only person who has not been able to make it in life. At least I was once offered education, and now I have a chance to further my education. What about those who have never been to school? What about those with deadly diseases? What about those who are disabled? Janet, you are awesome! I now see why we are friends. There is a great link between us. Like I said before, you know something that I know and I know something that you know. Thank you, dear friend, for telling me this special story. It has really changed the way I see my difficulties. I will tell it to others."

"You are welcome, Zulu."

"Janet, my only fears have always been that there are bad people wherever you are or go, and it has been because of those people that I am still left behind. I no longer know how to deal with them, to be honest with you."

"Zulu, listen: be strong and hang on. Temptations never end, jealousy never ends and problems never end, because nature is still alive and the world continues to live. You will meet temptations every day. There will be people who are jealous of you everywhere you go; problems will also follow you around. You have in mind only that it is a normality that cannot be stopped unless it stops by itself. All you have to do is to avoid temptations, disconnect from bad people who are always against you and solve problems where you can. No matter what people say, know that you have an objective to achieve. You came to this world for a reason and you should accomplish your mission. Remember that people are different, so you should be true to yourself. Winds will come, heavy rains will fall and you will need to be strong to hang on so that the winds and the rains do not take you away with them. Sunshine will come after that heavy weather, and you should be there to see that sunshine."

"Oh Janet, I love you so much. There is a reason why you came my way, my lovely friend," she sobbed.

"It's OK, my sweet friend. Same here – there is also a reason why you came my way. You have taught me so much and filled my book with amazing stories and poems."

"Now that I have finally found you, my good friend, trust me I will never let you go. My grandmother used to say, 'If you follow the footsteps of a good friend they will lead you to where she is sitting, and where she sits is surrounded with respect, peace, love, happiness, good people and intellectual art. And when you get there you too will sit like her.' Janet, I will follow your footsteps, and believe me I will get to where you are."

"You are already on your way, my dear friend," I smiled.

We hugged and then left the park to go back to her

place. She wanted me to see where she lived so I could get to know her family, and I agreed because I thought it was a good idea. She told me that I was the first person she had invited back to her home. I felt honoured. When we got there I was very surprised to see how beautiful her home was. The way she had spoken about it when she asked if she could come and take pictures at my place, it was like her home was no good. Her father was a wonderful man and her stepsisters and stepmother were wonderful too. She offered me a drink and said to me that all they had as food was Congolese cuisine. I said I would gladly have it. So I had cassava leaves in a spicy soup, and smoked goat with sweet spicy pepper on top of it and semolina on the side. Oh, I loved it! I was amazed to see how tasty Congolese cuisine was. I told Zulu that she should teach me one day how to cook the meal. The whole meal was perfect. Then she took me to her room, which was very neat and tidy. Not even a thing hanging around. She was a very clean girl. I was very happy to have found a young friend of my age who was just like me – apart from Stacey, who was thirteen years older than me. Later I had to go, because it was already 5.30 p.m., so she saw me off to the bus stop. We shook hands like warriors making peace with their opposition. It was like we had just met. Very funny.

"Keep on writing," she said.

"Keep on fighting," I replied.

Then I got on the bus, giving her a smile, and she smiled back.

Chapter 5

A week later Zulu called me on the phone, telling me how upset she was with Naomi and Tricia. She said that she was on her way to my house that morning. I told her to be quick about it because I was about to go out.

She did not look good when I saw her. Her eyes were all red, like somebody who has been crying all night. I became concerned and thought that what was bothering her must be very serious.

"I have to look good this weekend," she said. "I will get my hair done by Friday, get some fashionable clothes, some good make-up, and then get some pictures done and post them on Facebook. Yes, that is what I am going to do at the weekend so that all of these people who are mocking me on Facebook will see how pretty I can be. I don't care whether I have to finish all of the little savings I have. I just must do it."

"You have started again with this, Zulu. How many times do I have to tell you not to be bothered about what others are doing?"

"No, Janet, you don't understand! This time they have gone too far! Do you know what they did? I posted some pictures yesterday on my Facebook profile and they made some nasty comments on my pictures, saying 'not too good girl', 'go and get your hair done', 'don't force it, babes' … I mean, can you just imagine the embarrassment and humiliation? How could they do this to me? I am their friend."

"Zulu, you people with this issue of Facebook should stop making these comments that might hurt one another. Did you do anything similar to their photos?"

"No, Janet, I didn't, and that's what pains me the most. I always add good comments to their pictures, but see what I get in return? I am going to show them that they are nothing but nasty people!"

"Zulu, calm down. Let this Facebook thing go or it will make you mad. Concentrate on your English and maths classes for now. Let Tricia and Naomi be. Perhaps they don't know what they want in their lives. You at least know what you want."

"No, Janet, not when Spencer is also on Facebook and is friends with them too. You can imagine Spencer's reaction when seeing these girls' beautiful pictures all the time, while I can't even get a picture right."

"Are you in love with Spencer, or are you guys going out?"

"He said he loves me and I reciprocated. But I am afraid of losing him to Naomi. Naomi and Spencer are also friends on Facebook and you know how badly she likes him. She is always looking sexy and pretty. She posts pictures on her profile every day, and if you saw the number of likes on her pictures you wouldn't believe it! She often gets up to a hundred likes per picture and eighty-eight comments. I am going crazy. Spencer might become more attracted to her than he is to me. Don't you think so?"

"No, I don't think so. If he really loves you, Naomi's pictures will mean absolutely nothing to him. Listen, perhaps Naomi has many friends on Facebook and that's why her likes and comments are high. And why would Spencer want to dump you for her? She is not the only sexy-looking lady in the neighbourhood. Maybe I shouldn't be saying this, but I have to say it so that you understand: Naomi is not prettier than you are. Naomi is always looking sexy and beautiful because she spends every penny and every second looking after her body. She even borrows money when she's broke just to look good. So come on, Zulu, be yourself and don't try to be somebody else. I have already told you this several times. I guess Spencer loves you just the way you are."

"No, I don't believe in his love anymore. He's always liking and commenting on Naomi's pictures, so I am beginning to think that maybe he is in love with her, or maybe he doesn't want to ask her out because he knows that she has Kevin as a boyfriend."

"Listen, I believe that Spencer knows that Naomi loves him; and Spencer, knowing this, would have used this opportunity to go out with her a long time ago. So, my dear, I don't agree with you. He's just a friend to her, that's all."

"Well, if you say so."

"No, don't put it on me, love. I heard you once say that he also likes and comments on your pictures, so I see nothing to worry about. Or could it be Naomi who is looking for more attention from Spencer?"

"Yes, that is it! THAT – IS – IT! But that shouldn't make Spencer comment on her pictures all the time. I mean, I am his girlfriend and he should give me some respect and at the same time respect himself. Now look at how the girls have started mocking me. I wouldn't mind him commenting on some other girl's pictures, like Stacey, but definitely not Naomi or Tricia because they don't think like we do and they might think that he fancies one of them."

"Oh my God, you really are getting my head hot now with this Facebook issue. But I agree with you that by doing that he is degrading you somehow and at the same time he is degrading himself, so the best thing for you to do is to tell him to stop or he should put a limit on it. But please, Zulu, can we just forget about all this? You know the rules. Be who you are, Zulu, or you will go mad. You will turn into something else, and trust me, if you do, you will start doing things that you wouldn't have done in the first place and you will spoil your life."

"Janet, to be honest with you, I am going mad. I don't know how to control myself anymore. My fear is that he will fall in love with one of them and I don't want this to happen. But what do I do?"

"You don't need to do anything."

"Come on, Janet, don't give me that. You know there is really something I can do about this. See, Spencer is middle class, I am poor class, and Naomi and Tricia are middle class, too."

"Who told you that?"

"Naomi told me that she and Tricia are middle-class people; and the way I see Spencer, he could possibly be one, too."

"Ha-ha-ha, is that what Naomi told you about herself? Well, let me tell you that she's not middle class, and neither are you a poor-class person."

"She said she's intelligent and has a degree. You know she's very proud."

"I thought she said that she was also a lawyer. Did she tell you that, too?"

"No."

"Zulu, saying something does not really mean being it. Some people say lies to get themselves noticed and feel big. And some say lies to hide and protect their integrity or life so that nobody knows what they are doing or who they are. Bear this in mind."

"But Janet, when will this feeling of mine of being unable to look as pretty as I want end?"

"Listen, Zulu, be the best, no matter what you are or what you do. There is no top class in life, no middle class and no poor class. Everyone is working capital to this life (the fixed capital). No matter what you are or what you do, be the best. Be happy in what you are and do not think that those higher than you are happier or greater than you. They are higher than you but they are not the best at what they do. If you are not good in maths, be the best in English. People will see this quality in you; the mathematician will come to you, asking you to read his reports to check if the grammar in them is correct. Zulu, you have taught me that there are many intelligent people all around the world. Many of them never went to school or received a higher education, but they are seen to be the best at what they do because those who attend school still go to them for help."

"Oh Janet, I love you so much. Thank you for that. I feel a bit more in control now."

"By trying to copy Tricia and Naomi you will end up inhabiting their world."

"Thanks again, my good friend."

"No, don't thank me. You already know all this and I really shouldn't be repeating myself. You are just being stubborn, that's all."

"I know, and I am sorry."

"It's OK. So can we put all this Facebook thing behind us?"

"Yeah, sure. So what are you up to?"

"I am going to the local library to do some research for my book."

"Can I come with you?"

"Shouldn't you be at college today?"

"I don't like my maths teacher. He is always picking on me."

"Are you telling me you skipped college today? No, I don't believe you. He's picking on you because he wants you to learn. Or is it because of Facebook?"

"Janet, I am sorry. I didn't mean to."

"Zulu, just rush to college now. If you are late, apologise to your maths teacher for being late."

"OK, I will do that. But please don't be mad at me."

"I am not. You just go now."

In the library, as I was doing my research, I had the idea of opening a Facebook account in order to see for myself what really goes on there. And so I opened one that evening at home. I added a few of the friends I knew. I posted a few pictures of mine which I had always had on my camera. I was surprised to see how all of the friends I had added liked my pictures and made great comments. Then I saw again about thirty friend requests just for that first day. I was beginning to understand Zulu's position about Facebook. But there was no better advice I could have given Zulu than to be herself and that her own time would come. Then I thought of writing something moral to her, so I sent her a message on Facebook: "Zulu, I now understand how you feel about Facebook. Earlier on this morning when we talked about it you asked me what you should do, and my answer now is this – make the most of every day. Work hard every day, yet do the best you can to make your day happy. I do not mean that you should do bad things, but good things that will please you and those around you. If you make the best of every day you will not care about what happens tomorrow. It is the same if, every day, you keep your house clean, your room tidy and your backyard mowed; you will not worry about who comes to see you tomorrow. You may only miss one day of cleaning your house, but this will be the day that you will receive guests and they might think something else of you. You may be late only on the day of your job interview, but the interviewer might think it is your habit. You may only walk with a criminal once, but people will think that you do so frequently, and may think that you are also a criminal. Do not let people think of you as something you are not. Don't show people that you don't have enough to look good or that you would rather save your money for important things than look good. Instead show them that you do have enough. So, for example, if you have £5, use £2 to buy shampoo and conditioner to wash and tidy your hair, then keep £3 for your savings. And do not forget that your own time will come when you will have everything you want."

Via email I also sent Zulu a story from my book – *Louis and Mark: When My Sun Shines I Will Rise*:

Louis and Mark were good friends whose friendship started when they met at a hostel.

Louis was a very good person who thought that he had found a good friend just like him when he first met Mark.

Louis loved his studies very much. He had nothing great to show people, but he was proud of his studies and knew that with them, one day, he would achieve something good in life.

When Louis noticed that Mark was not the type of friend he had believed, Louis started to withdraw, but, for reasons that have never been clear, Mark would not leave Louis alone.

While they were living at the hostel, Mark started to become jealous of Louis. He started to tell Louis that he should stop reading and get himself a job, as Mark had done. Fortunately, Louis was smart, and every time Mark made this suggestion, Louis responded that his studies were a priority to him.

Mark made money easily, and sometimes Louis wondered where he was getting it from, but thank God he never asked or tried to go with him.

Every time Mark entered Louis's room he would say, "Louis, you have nothing in your room. Why don't you buy this or that to put in here?"

Louis would respond, "The time will come for me to put anything I like in my room; it is not only to be a room but a house."

Mark laughed at Louis every time he heard this. Louis knew what he wanted; he knew what he was doing, he had an objective and he was convinced that through his studies he would someday become more important. He never thought of following Mark to find out what he did or how he earned his money. His friendship with Mark existed only at the hostel or when they went shopping. Other than inside the hostel and while they shopped, Louis didn't go anywhere with Mark. Louis spent his time reading or going out with his fiancée.

Sometimes, when Mark visited Louis in his room, he tried to persuade Louis to stop reading, go with him and do what he did. However, what Mark did not understand was that Louis's education and intelligence was given to him as a gift when he was born.

Louis's response to Mark was, "I do not make money the way you do. I do not make dirty money. When my sun shines, I will rise. What I mean by this is that when I have finished my studies I will get a good job and I will make proper money."

Every time Louis said this to Mark, his friend looked back at him strangely. Louis could not explain why Mark looked at him that way. He wondered if Mark wanted to destroy his life or his dedication. Was it because he knew that Louis would have a bright future and was jealous of it, or was it because he had no future and wanted the same for Louis? No answers were forthcoming.

Louis always stayed true to himself, no matter the level of pain, discomfort and lies or the traps that Mark set for him. He never changed. He knew that when his sun shone he would rise and prove his adversaries wrong.

While Mark was only thinking of money, money and

more money, Louis was progressing as usual. Louis left the hostel to get away from Mark's bad attitude. He went somewhere else, to a new city where he lived happily. He finished his studies and became a lawyer, earning a very good income just as he had wished. Today Louis has succeeded in his life by staying loyal to himself, his studies and his ambitions. He has two beautiful children (a boy and a girl) and a very good wife.

For many years after Louis had left the hostel, he didn't hear anything about Mark. Surprisingly, the first time he heard his name after all that time was on the TV news. Mark had been jailed for thirty years after robbing a bank. Louis just laughed and praised God, but there was one question he never got the answer to: why was Mark against him, his studies and his ambitions? Only Mark, the prisoner, could answer this question.

Later Zulu responded to my message, asking me if what I had told her about 'making the most of every day' was what I also did myself, and I replied by saying yes. I told her that even when she got to have enough to look after herself she shouldn't show off like other people did, because you shouldn't make yourself known to people but let people notice you. As soon as I clicked on the 'send' button, my husband, George and Christopher walked in from work. George was looking very sad and I wondered what was going on. I stood up from the computer desk and offered them seats. Then I offered them hot drinks.

George started saying, "Had I listened to you, John, this wouldn't have happened to me. I can't believe that she was only a cheat and a gold-digger. She has squandered my money with all of her so-called tenderness. She really meant the world to me, but not anymore. She has been cheating on me with some other guys. Had I not caught her today she would have denied it again. I have been blind and stupid."

"Calm down, George, you are not the only one. Naomi has done the same thing to me, too," said Christopher.

I was shocked to hear that Naomi had had an affair with Christopher too.

"You are joking, Christopher? You mean you, too? Gosh, these girls are demons," said George. "They must have worked us out. Shit. I am going to call Tricia right now and tell her that the marriage is off."

"Are you telling me that you were going to carry on with the marriage after all she has done to you?" said Christopher. "Come on, don't be silly, George."

"And you, Chris, who knew about your affair with Naomi? When did you guys start or finish? Why is my own concern here," said George.

"Listen, I never proposed to Naomi or got engaged to her. I take my love stuff very slowly and don't rush myself like you did," said Christopher.

My husband stepped in. "It is OK. Let's calm down and not make things worse here. George, you have already had enough arguments with Tricia – calling her to tell her that will make your mood even worse. Just text her and tell her you are calling the marriage off. And as for you, Christopher, just forget about Naomi, since you never intended to marry her anyway … Forget about them and move on with your lives, OK?"

All of a sudden I became worried about my friendships with Naomi and Tricia. After all that had been discussed by my husband and his friends, I started seeing these two girls as gold-diggers and troublemakers. Tricia once told me that her way to a man's wallet was the way she made love to him, and so did Naomi. I guess George and Christopher might have been blinded by the two girls' tenderness and love-making. But for how long would the girls continue like this? Was it all about how to make love? Or did the manners and character of a woman count the most? I believe it is not all about love-making, because Charles, who is also my husband's friend, refused to have anything to do with either of them, meaning that the character of a woman is of utmost importance to a man. For me a woman could always learn how to make love to her man at one time or another. But **good character** is something that you cannot learn to have with one click or at one time because it is something you grow up with from being a child to an adult.

The next day my feelings about the girls faded away completely. I became eager to cut off the friendship with them as soon as possible, but I didn't know how to do it. The more I ran away from them, the closer they became. George had cancelled all the marriage plans. He told my husband how broke Tricia had left him. My husband just couldn't believe that George could do this to himself. As a solicitor, George should have gotten himself a decent young lady rather than breaking his heart and his reputation with some nasty girl like Tricia. It was a shame to see how George and Tricia ended after all the plans they had ahead of them. I thought she was for real. But then I didn't like prejudging and I wanted to hear from Tricia for myself. I didn't like asking after people's affairs because it was none of my business.

To my great surprise Tricia called me and started telling me how bad George had been to her.

When I asked in what way he had been bad to her, she laughed, saying, "The stupid pig became obsessed with me and wanted to have me around him all the time. Can you imagine? He had never tasted anything like me before. The more he ate me the hungrier he became, poor man. But seriously, where am I going to go with a pig like him? I just wanted to get some cash out of him, that's all. So how is he? Is he still crying a lot? Still depressed? Oh, poor man." She laughed. "I hope he is not finding comfort at your place. If he's there with you people, tell him to take heart and move on."

"This is not good, Tricia. This is not how you do things. I am not finding it funny at all," I replied.

At that point I decided to end my friendships with Naomi and Tricia. We stopped seeing each other.

Chapter 6

The weeks passed, and at midnight on Sunday 15 February 2009 I started having contractions every three to five minutes. I woke my husband and we called the hospital and were told that I should have a deep bath first and to call back if the pain continued. So my husband took me to the bathroom. After soaking in the bath for five minutes, with only my head out of the water, the pain stopped. I preferred to stay in the bath rather than in bed so that I didn't feel the pain. I asked my husband to make me a cup of tea. My husband made me a cup of tea and brought it into the bathroom. He went back to bed and told me to shout his name whenever I needed him. After thirty minutes in the bath I decided to come out of the bath and go back to bed. Ten minutes after leaving the bathroom the pain started again at an increased level, but I decided to live with it this time. I tried to cope with the pain but it got to the point where I couldn't cope with it any longer, so we had to call the hospital back and they asked us to go in. This was around 4 a.m., meaning I had been in labour for four hours.

In the delivery suite at the hospital I was given some pain-relief tablets, but they didn't work. I was screaming. My husband couldn't bear to see me that way. I asked him to be strong. My parents were on holiday in the Bahamas and were supposed to be back on 17 February, before my due date. My due date was 25 February, but I gave birth earlier because of the walking I had started doing at my local park. Later, around 8 a.m., I called Stacey, but she didn't pick up. It was the same thing when I called Zulu. I guess they were either busy or still sleeping. Then I received a phone call, thinking it was a call back from Zulu or Stacey. I asked my husband to pick up as I was in severe pain. When I heard my husband say, "Hello Naomi," I wondered why she was calling and, if she was aware of my situation, who had told her. Then my husband said, "It's Naomi. She's just checking on you to see if you are OK."

"Tell her that I'm at Hillingdon Hospital, maternity ward," I said with a weak tone of voice. I guess I needed more people around me.

She was there in less than twenty minutes. She asked me why I hadn't told her I was in labour, saying that had she not called me she wouldn't have known. I didn't say anything other than sorry. Later Zulu called and apologised for not being able to pick up, saying that she had been having her bath to get ready for church. Stacey too called and said that her phone had been on silent. They were both on their way to see me. Naomi gave me all the support a friend could give her fellow friend. My husband had left the hospital to go home to make something special for me to eat. Naomi stayed with me all this time. Later I felt like eating green apples but was too exhausted to call my husband to ask him to bring me some, so I asked Naomi to call my husband for me using my phone. Naomi was really a great help to me that day. I was astonished about all that she had done for me.

The next day I was discharged from hospital. My parents were told by my husband about my situation. They took the next flight to London. They were so worried and couldn't wait to see me and my little girl. When they finally arrived at my place I was very happy to see them. It's good to see a mum helping out her daughter and caring for the granddaughter. My mum decided to stay at my place for some time just to help me out with my newborn. What could I ever have done without my mother? She would cook all our meals, help me clean the house and the garden – in fact, she was doing all the housework and I was having a lot of rest, as she demanded.

Naomi continued paying me visits. She paid me more visits than Stacey, Zulu or Tricia. She would help me do the laundry. She even asked me to think of anything she could do to be of help, but I told her not to worry – that my mum was already doing the housework for me. Naomi visited me every day. I was very happy with the way Naomi had changed the negative side of her. She became my closest friend, as she was always coming to my house to check that my little girl and I were OK. My mum came to like her, but my husband still could not warm to her. I did not understand why.

Zulu became a bit jealous, but more worried, when she saw that Naomi and I had become that close. Zulu would always tell me to be careful. I guess she felt a bit left out, so she decided to put some distance between us so that I could feel happy being friends with Naomi. Zulu didn't want to make me uncomfortable with her warnings. I was sad because I liked Zulu so much, but Naomi couldn't let me go.

Tricia also sometimes paid me a visit and brought gifts for the baby.

Chapter 7

It took me more than a year after giving birth to start suspecting that what my husband had been telling me about Tricia and Naomi was true.

One day Naomi came to visit me and asked me if I would go with her and visit one of her friends. When she came to my house I was cleaning the house. I was still in my pyjamas and had not had my bath yet. My husband had gone out shopping with our little girl. I told her to make herself at home in the living room, offered her hot chocolate with some chocolate-chip cookies and told her to wait for me there while I had my bath. I walked upstairs and into the bathroom. As I started bathing, I heard footsteps that sounded like somebody walking up the stairs, but I couldn't be very sure because of the shower tap flowing.

I turned off the tap. "John, is that you? Are you back so soon?"

There was no answer. I thought that it was just my imagination, so I continued having my bath.

Then the bathroom door opened. I was frightened and said, "Who is that?"

"It's just me, Naomi. I came to use the toilet."

"But there is a toilet downstairs and you know it."

"Oh, I am sorry. I completely forgot that there is a toilet downstairs too."

"You are not serious, Naomi, are you?"

"Oh, come on, Janet, I just told you that I forgot."

But that was not all. She opened the shower curtain by force and went, "Wow! What a beautiful body you have, Janet. Huh, your husband is very lucky to have you, dear."

"Get out of here now," I shouted. "I mean it!"

111

She quickly went out of the bathroom and ran back to the living room. I was no longer interested in having my bath. I put on my towel and rushed straight to the living room. She was just sitting there.

I was seething. "Do you realise what you have just done?"

"Janet, please forget about it. I said I am sorry."

"I just don't believe you."

"I am very sorry."

"You can't do that, you understand me? Let it be the first and last time you will ever do a thing like that. Have I made myself clear?"

"Janet, do you know that you are very pretty? I get obsessed with you at times, you know. Please try to understand."

"You must be out of your mind."

"No, I am serious."

"I am beginning to doubt your identity."

"No, let's not go there; I am not what you are thinking I am. Listen … OK, let's just forget about all this."

"No, seriously, I have to tell you that I am beginning to think that your friendship with me is for something."

"OK, good, I will answer that – you are so pretty and I like you and I don't like your husband because he's ten years older than you and he makes things so difficult for us. I can't take you out clubbing because he wouldn't let us go, but if you had a young husband we all would have got along very well."

"I have told you before never to bring my husband or his age into anything that has to do with me and you!"

"What I am saying is that your husband is much older than you are. Don't get me wrong, babe, I am not saying that your man is old. He has no six pack and you have a great body. You know the match is not too perfect."

"You really have nothing to say, do you? You are just confusing yourself!"

"Oh, come on … Don't you worry, by the time we get to see the person we are going to see today you will understand what I mean."

"Let me tell you – maybe you don't know. Out of a hundred men who asked me out I chose only one, and that man happens to be my husband. Among those hundred men were plenty of handsome guys with six packs, but only one man caught my attention, meaning I don't go for looks but for brains. I look for how clever, respectable and humble a man is and not how cute he is."

"Alright, girl. Sorry I brought this up with you. Please forgive me."

"What are you doing?"

"I am apologising to you."

"I didn't ask you to get on your knees."

"Well, this could be the only way to show you how sorry I am."

"Please just stand up. And don't you ever bring this up again. I will forget it because you are my friend."

"Thank you."

"And for your information, I am no longer interested in accompanying you to see your friend."

"Oh babes, why? Is it because of what I have just done?"

"Good that you have got the answer by yourself. You are on your own."

Then she changed the subject. She started telling me about her birthday – that she was organising her birthday party at her place and I was invited.

I said, "Good, we will see to that when the time comes."

"Oh please," she said, "you have to be there. It's in a

week's time and I have already finalised all the arrangements, so I have already prepared everything."

A week after it was Naomi's birthday; she turned twenty nine. It was April 2010. I didn't go because I was just not keen to go. Then I heard from Stacey that Naomi had also invited Stacey and Zulu. Zulu did attend the party but Stacey didn't. Something happened at the party which Zulu later described to me, as follows.

Naomi had an odd conversation with Spencer.

"Oh, hi Spencer," she said.

"Oh, Naomi … Hi."

"So what's up? I mean, what are you doing outside when everybody is inside?"

"Nothing really, just chilling with my beer … getting some fresh air."

"Huh."

"Nice party by the way; and you are looking great."

"Oh thank you. Eh-eh …"

"You are welcome. Alright, see you. I will just go back in."

"Eh-eh, Spencer …"

"Yeah?"

"Wait – can I tell you something?"

Naomi remained silent for a few seconds.

"What is it, Naomi?" said Spencer. "Is there anything wrong?"

"Eh-eh, yes, but you will have to keep it a secret."

"A secret? Is it that bad?"

"Yes. Eh-eh …"

"Listen, Naomi, if there is something you think I should know then say it, because I am running out of patience. If you think it's not that important then keep it to yourself."

"Why are you always harsh on me, and not on …?"

"And not on who? Anyway, I got to go in. Thanks,

114

by the way."

"OK, OK. Listen. You know that girl – the girl you have been kissing lately …"

"That girl hasn't got a name?"

"That African girl called Zulu – who you were kissing."

"Oh, so you do know her name? And what about her?"

"For how long have you guys been dating?"

"Why?"

"Anyway … Stop dating her."

"And why, Miss know-it-all?"

"Why do you call me that? I am telling you this because I don't want you to break your heart. She sleeps around with lots of men. I even heard that it's possible that she might have a deadly disease. She had several abortions back in Africa. I know everything about her. She's no good."

"Anything else I should know?"

"She snatched my boyfriend away from me … And she …"

"Oh, stop it! Stop the crap, you slut! Shame on you! You think I don't know what you girls do sometimes behind your friends' backs? You go around telling lies about your friends simply because you don't truly love one another and you are so jealous!"

"No, I am serious, Spencer. You can even ask Tricia."

"I should ask Tricia? That one again? Your personal secretary, whom you make up stories with as if they were real stories? When are you guys going to change your lifestyles? Grow up!"

"Believe me, Spencer …"

"Oh, shut the fuck up! You are jealous, that's all. I can't believe you! I heard you say once that she's one of your best friends and that she was a good friend, and now you have suddenly changed your story simply because you believe that by changing your story I will personally get my mind off her. Hell no, that's not going to happen. See, that's where you are mistaking yourself, because I am in love with this girl. And maybe you don't know, but if there is anybody hiding something here, it is you. I mean, how do you do it, Naomi? Tell me. How do you make up all these untrue stories about people? Where do you get the imagination from? Unless you are the one who is sleeping around or who has secrets that you are hiding? Perhaps we should know?"

"Spencer, are you calling me a liar?"

"Yes, Naomi, that's what you are! You are a very BIG LIAR! I know my girl Zulu. She's so lovely and I will have her!"

"I just don't want you to get hurt …"

"Thank you, but let me find out for myself!"

"Spencer, wait … I mean, how can you date an African girl? She's not even that pretty."

"Ah, really? It's no longer a problem to do with Zulu. It's now a problem to do with me and my choice of girl. And who ever told you that you were pretty, anyway? Do you know what, Naomi, any man who ever said that you were pretty misled you by telling you a lie so that he could have his way with you. Naomi, you are the ugliest lady I have ever met in my whole life! And one more thing before I go – don't you ever come near me ever again. You might have succeeded in destroying other couples, but this time your poison has failed. Bad friend! You should be ashamed of yourself!"

"Spencer … OK, I am sorry. But, please, can I say something else to you, please?"

"Not another word from you! Bitch! I am out of this party!"

"Spencer, you called me a bitch!"

"That's what you are!"

"Spencer, wait. Please, wait. I love you so much that I ..."

That was how Spencer left the party.

The following day was the day Zulu came to tell me about what had happened at the party. She rang me early in the morning; she sounded very angry. I told her to come down to my house so we could talk about whatever it was that was eating her up. Minutes later someone rang the doorbell and I knew it was her. She walked in with tears rolling down her cheeks. I asked her what the matter was. She responded that somebody was trying to destroy her life.

I told her to stop wandering around and to sit down. "Would you like a drink before you start telling me what's eating you up?"

"Yes, something really cold please, eh-eh, water would be fine."

I got her a glass of cold water. She drank it in five seconds.

"Zulu, take it easy, please. You are getting me very worried."

She started explaining what had happened at the party. Spencer had told her everything that Naomi had said about her. Zulu told me that a similar thing had happened to her once before, back in Africa. This was her story:

When I was eighteen years old there was this young lady who came to buy peanuts from me and my grandmother at the local market. This lady became a regular customer and then a friend. Her name was Mandarina. Mandarina came to love me a lot, claiming that I was a wise and good-hearted friend. She called me her 'best friend'. Mandarina drew closer and closer to me. At times she would come and help me and my grandmother sell the peanuts. My grandmother came to like Mandarina as her own granddaughter. But then something happened.

One day my grandmother was very ill and was admitted to hospital as an inpatient. I had no choice but to close the business for the time being so I could look after her at the hospital. Mandarina said that she would help me and keep the business running for me while I looked after my grandmother until she got out of hospital. I was very happy to see that she was trying to help me, so I agreed. While I was at the hospital looking after my grandmother, Mandarina was able to make good sales and good profits. At the end of every working day Mandarina paid us a visit at the hospital and gave me the whole revenue from the day's sales. I was very happy with Mandarina and the commitment she had shown in helping me and my grandmother, so I gave her some money for each day she worked for me. Giving her some money was the only way to show my gratitude. But later she refused to share the profits with me, saying that she didn't want anything from me. Being paid made her uncomfortable, because she was doing what she was doing for me was because I was her best friend. I still remember her exact words: "Zulu, I am doing what I am doing for you and your grandmother because you are my best friend." I was joyful to see that I had a good friend like Mandarina.

My grandmother improved and a few days later she was discharged from hospital, but the doctor recommended that she continue with her prescriptions. On our way home I bought vegetables, fish, beef, chicken, goat, yam and plantain together with some soft drinks. When we got home I made a special meal for my grandmother but also to thank my friend Mandarina for helping us out all this time. When I had finished cooking I set the table and left to fetch Mandarina, who was still working on the stall at the market.

Mandarina was very surprised to see me. "Zulu – what are you doing here? Is your grandmother OK?"

"Yes, she's OK. In fact the doctor said that she's fine now and that we could go home," I replied.

"So you mean that grandma is at home!" she shouted with joy.

I smiled and answered her with a big, "Yes!"

Mandarina was very happy to hear that my grandmother was well again.

"Let's close for the day," I said. "I want you to come home with me."

"But we haven't finished for the day and we would lose a lot of profits," she answered with a sad face.

"It's OK, Mandarina. I just want to celebrate grandma's return. Her good health means a lot to me, so I just want us to take a day off and be happy."

"OK, if you say so," she replied.

When we got home Mandarina was very surprised to see that I had cooked all those different meals for just the three of us. We ate, drank, laughed and danced. It was a happy day for the three of us. When we had finished enjoying ourselves I asked Mandarina to follow me to our bedroom (where my grandmother and I slept).

When we got there, I said, "Mandarina, you say that I am your best friend, right?"

"You are my only best friend, Zulu," she confirmed.

"So, can I trust you?"

"Oh, sure you can."

"Mandarina, I have always wanted to go back to school, but it's been very difficult for me to achieve that and at the same time sell peanuts at the local market. Basically, what I am saying is this: I have been able to save a good amount of money to further my education, and I want you to do the same for yourself. So I thought that I would give the profits that you made for me while I was at the hospital to you so you can use the money to further your education, and I will use the savings I made for myself since I started the business. Come, let me show you where I hide my savings. I hide my money in this little box under my bed. So take your own share."

"Zulu, I have already told you not to worry yourself. You don't need to do that."

"No, I insist, Mandarina. Please take it. Education is very important and I want you too to further your education," I begged her.

"OK – if you insist. But thank you very much. Zulu, you are the only best friend I have," she sobbed.

"It's good to hear that again, Mandarina," I smiled.

Later, Mandarina left for her house. She lived with her mum and aunties. The next day she came back to my house and told me that there was this guy in our village who was deeply in love with me and that she had already spoken with the guy about me. She told me that the guy was looking for a wife to marry, and he saw me to be the only young lady in the whole village who was competent and decent enough to be his wife. I was very excited at first, because this was the very first time for me finding out about love, so when Mandarina told me this I felt something sweet in my heart, something soft and beautiful. I told Mandarina to tell the guy that he should tell me himself about his feelings for me, and she promised to do that. The next day she brought him to my house. I was shaking and didn't know what to do. I offered them some drinks that were left over from my grandmother's little party.

He asked Mandarina to excuse us for a while, but I said no, it was OK for her to stay with us. So he started telling me how much time he spent observing my character and my hard work and that I was amazing and very fit to be his wife. I said to him that I hoped he was not just flattering me. He said he wasn't, and that was why he had come to tell me to my face. I was so happy to hear that from him, because as a Christian my faith did not allow me to have anything to do with a man before marriage. So he promised to come back the next day and said that I should talk to my grandmother in advance, and so I did.

When he came back the next day, I had prepared some good food for him. He spoke with my grandmother and we concluded everything about our traditional marriage. All that was left for me to do was let my mother and father's relatives know about it and get their consent before we proceeded with the marriage.

The following day Mandarina came to my house, telling me that her mum was celebrating her birthday party that weekend at their place and that I was invited. I told her that it was OK by me – I would be there for her. Then she wanted to spend the day in my house and I told her that it was OK by me and that she could stay with my grandmother, but I had to go and announce my marriage proposal to my mum and my father's relatives. My mission for that day was accomplished; my father's brother then requested that Tony, my husband to be, go there himself and ask for my hand in marriage. So I went straight to Tony to tell him what they had said and he agreed that we would both go there on Sunday. I was very happy that our marriage preparations were going so smoothly.

It was Saturday and it was Mandarina's mum's birthday. By this time I had resumed work at the market selling peanuts. I closed the business early to prepare for the birthday party. I rushed home and went straight into the bedroom and reached under the bed to get my brown box of money, but I couldn't see it. I searched the whole house, thinking I might have misplaced it, but it was nowhere to be found. I started crying and asked my grandmother if she had seen the box, but she said that she had not. I was running out of patience and out of time. I was worried as to how I would be able to continue with my grandmother's prescriptions if I didn't find my money box, and I was worried how I would get the money to buy a party dress and a birthday gift for Mandarina's mum. After all the good things Mandarina had done for me and my grandmother I wanted to be there for her.

I panicked and didn't know what to do, so I went to see a neighbour called 'Lady Beauty', a fancy lady who always kept herself up to date with fashion: a gold-digger, a smoker and a thief. She had named herself Lady Beauty in the belief that she was the only fine-looking lady in our village. Although I knew that Lady Beauty was not the right person to ask for help, I went to her anyway. I knocked at her door. It took her about three minutes to come to the door. She opened the door with a cigarette in her hands and asked me to come in; at the same time I started coughing, as I couldn't bear the smoke. I told her why I was there: that I needed a very nice party dress to wear to a party. Lady told me that I had to pay a price. I asked her to name her price and said that I was willing to pay it, because I couldn't miss the party because Mandarina had been there for me when I was in trouble.

"Did you just say Mandarina?" she asked me.

"Yes, Mandarina. Do you know her?"

"That girl is trouble … Anyway, you have to pay me some cash first before I can give you a party dress."

I told her that I had no cash with me; I hadn't been able to sell any peanuts that day. I promised to pay her the £5 she asked for in three days' time. Lady agreed to this and lent me a nice pink dress and a pink pair of shoes.

I was very happy that I had managed to get a dress and shoes, but one other thing kept me worrying: a birthday gift for Mandarina's mum. Business had been bad that day and I had very little money, so I thought I should take peanuts with me to the party instead. I washed my hair, dressed up and left for the party. When I got there I was very happy to see that there were no peanuts on the party-food table, so I added my dish of peanuts to the table. I was very happy to see Mandarina smiling at me and I thought it was a good sign. However, I still apologised to Mandarina for not being able to get her mum a proper gift. I told her that it was because something had happened and I had been left with insufficient money but that I would explain the whole thing to her after the party. Mandarina insisted that she was OK with the gift of peanuts and told me that the main reason for having her mum's birthday party was because she wanted to attract a guy and get him to fall in love with her. She said that she had spent all the money I had given to her on the party.

I was shocked. "Is that not a stupid thing you have done? What about furthering your education as we agreed? Education is very important."

But she didn't give me an answer.

I asked her who the guy in question was and whether he was at the party. She said he was too shy and that they were going to meet up later in private.

"OK," I said. "Just be wise in everything you are doing."

I tried as best as I could to keep my mood happy, as it was my friend's mum's party, but I couldn't stop thinking of how my money had just vanished like that. I had also invited Tony along and he hadn't turned up, so there was a lot going on in my head. I was asking myself so many questions.

Four hours later I told Mandarina that I had to go, as my grandmother needed me. Mandarina thanked me for coming and for offering her mum peanuts as a gift. She said that their guests had really enjoyed them. You are welcome, I said. You are my best friend, said Mandarina. Thank you, I said, and then left. But I didn't go straight home because I wanted to know why Tony had disappointed me in not coming to pick me up as we agreed so we could both go to the party.

I went to his house and knocked at the door. There was no answer, but I could see lights on in the front windows. I knocked again but there was still no answer. So I waited at the door. After waiting for two hours I saw him coming back with a lady. It was too dark to see who this lady was – in Africa we don't really have streetlights like we have here in the UK. As soon as they noticed me sitting there on the floor the lady stopped walking and refused to get closer and she left.

I asked Tony where he had been and why he hadn't turned up as we agreed. He just said to me that he had been very busy. I asked him why the lights were on in his house. Was it a way to tell me that he was in when he wasn't in? But he wouldn't answer me – he just opened his door, leaving me behind.

I held the door with my two hands. "Tony, what is going on? Is there anything I should know? We have a plan to meet my father's relatives tomorrow, and acting this way won't accomplish that."

He told me that there were no more plans between us and that he could not marry a prostitute like me.

I couldn't believe my ears. "Me, a prostitute? Have you forgotten that I am a virgin?"

He said that I was a bloody liar. He had found a beautiful woman to marry and he couldn't marry a witch like me. He closed the door on me.

I cried my eyes out. I demanded to know who had told him all these lies. I cried and cried, but he wouldn't open the door to me. I kept on crying until I realised that I was just hurting myself and it was getting very late.

My grandmother was worried. She hadn't slept, because it was my first time coming home that late and she thought something bad had happened to me. When I got home I cried on my grandmother's shoulders. We both cried and cried. She told me that it was OK and that we should leave the rest to God Almighty – that He would fight our enemies for us. I cried all night. The next morning, as I continued crying, I searched the house again for my money but couldn't find anything. I cried out loud. Why was this happening to me? I left to see Tony again. We'd had a plan to execute on that day, and my grandmother insisted that I go and talk to him again, saying that perhaps he had just had a bad day.

So there I was again in front of his door. I knocked and knocked but there was no answer. I stayed there for five hours, until I couldn't wait any longer. I left to see my father's relatives and explained to them what was happening to me. They refused to believe me and said that I was a bad girl and that I had made a fool of them because they had already prepared all that was needed to receive me and Tony. I tried explaining that it was not my fault. I even went down on my knees. But they chased me out of their compound, saying that I was nothing but a disgrace to them and that I had dishonoured them. They wouldn't even believe my story. So I went back home to give all the details of my journey to my grandmother. My pain was too much, and I had to seek Mandarina for comfort. I went to see her at her place on that same Sunday. She was so cold with me. I told her all about what had happened, from the disappearance of my money box to the disappointment of Tony. All she said was that everything would be fine and that I should go home and she would come to see me later in the day, as she had a crucial appointment to attend. I said that I would be waiting for her, but she never came. The next morning I decided to leave home early to go and get peanuts from my suppliers so I could try to raise some profits that day, because the little peanuts I was left with were not enough to make a good profit. After visiting the wholesalers I left for the market and started selling. I had to be strong despite my sadness, because I had to think of my grandmother's health and my future as well. Unfortunately, business was no good that day. I became worried about how I was going to pay back the wholesalers and Lady Beauty. The following day business was bad again, so I decided to go and see Mandarina to see if she could help me with some funds to pay my debts. I told her I would reimburse her as soon as I had made a profit, but Mandarina said that she couldn't help me because she had to buy herself some gold earrings and she couldn't wait to have them. I begged her. Couldn't the jewellery wait, I asked? I had to pay someone back. I only had a day left to get the money and I was afraid that if I didn't pay the person back as we had agreed they might harm me. She still refused to help me. I left quietly. I didn't want to make a big deal out of it. I didn't even tell Mandarina that I had borrowed a dress and a pair of shoes just to please her and her mum when I attended their party.

The next day I didn't want to go and sell my peanuts at the market, because I just saw that it was going to be like the other days where I couldn't sell anything, but my grandmother insisted that I go. So I finally left for the market. To my great surprise business was very good that day. I was able to make a good profit. So after I closed I went to pay my suppliers and then I went to pay my debt to Lady Beauty. I knocked at her door and this time it took her no longer than a minute to open the door. I knew she was expecting me. She asked me to come in, but I said no, I was in a hurry and had just come to pay her what I owed. So I gave her the money and I also gave her back the dress and the shoes, telling her that I had already washed the dress for her and cleaned the shoes.

She was very touched. "You are the first person to whom I have lent a dress who has washed the dress and cleaned the shoes. I must say I am impressed. Can I tell you something?"

"Yes, sure, go on."

"Have you lost some money? Money in a wooden box?"

My heart started beating faster. "Yes, yes! Have you seen it anywhere?"

She wasn't happy with the way I was panicking. She asked me to come into her house, saying that she wanted to tell me something, but I was afraid to go in. I begged her just to tell me at the door. She said she would, on the condition that I stopped shouting, because I could draw the attention of her neighbours. I said fine, I wouldn't shout again. Then she told me that my money box had been stolen by Mandarina and that she had come to Lady and asked Lady to hide the wooden box for her. Mandarina told Lady that she had never liked me. She had always been jealous of my hard work and was happy to have snatched my husband to be, Tony.

I couldn't believe all that Lady Beauty was telling me and asked her for proof. She asked me to wait where I was and she went to collect the wooden box Mandarina had given her to hide. When she came back with the box, tears started rolling down my cheeks. I asked Lady if in fact she had stolen the box and was just pretending that it was Mandarina. She asked me how she was to know that I had a secret box of money. Then she wanted to give me more proof.

"If you doubt me," she said, "take this wooden box and go to Tony's house now. That is where she is at the moment. You ask her for yourself and see what she says."

I took the box and rushed to Tony's house like a mad person. To my great surprise they were both sitting in the compound, cuddling and kissing each other. As I got closer I asked God to give me self-control. I didn't want to bother myself about why she had snatched my man from me; I just wanted to know why she had stolen my money. When had I wronged her?

When they saw me they both played the innocent. They acted as if they hadn't hurt me in any way.

With tears in my eyes, I said, "Mandarina, did you steal this box and then give it to Lady Beauty to hide for you?"

"Who told you that?"

"Lady Beauty did."

"It's a lie. I didn't steal your money."

Then I heard a voice behind me. "Then who did it, Mandarina? Are you denying that you brought this box to me to hide for you and you paid me to do it?" It was Lady Beauty – she must have followed me there.

Mandarina was speechless. I asked her to say something about it, but she said nothing, not even a word. I went crazy. I asked her how I had wronged her and what I had done to deserve all this. I told her that Lady Beauty had told me everything she had said about me. Mandarina still wouldn't say anything. I just looked at them both and said, "God will judge my case for me," and then I left. I decided not to have anything more to do with any girl from my village. Mandarina was so jealous of my good reputation. Some people come to you pretending to be your friend when that is anything but their real intention. They see you always shining brightly and their sole mission is to destroy your life.

After Zulu had finished telling me her story about her own experience with friends, I was very shocked to see how wicked people can be at times. Zulu promised herself that she would never have anything to do with Naomi again. I became concerned about Naomi, because everybody was complaining about her wicked ways. I did have a feeling about it myself, too, and yet I still took her in as my friend. She was there for me when I gave birth. She gave me all the support I needed. I couldn't easily rip her off my friends' list, so I let her be.

Chapter 8

In June 2010 I went to France to visit my husband's family. I spent a week in Paris with them. It was great, and I had great fun; I especially enjoyed the food. When I came back home to London something very bad was awaiting me.

Twelve hours after arriving home my house phone rang.

It was Stacey. "Hello, Janet, darling. How are you?"

"I am fine. And you?"

"I am OK, dear. How was your holiday?"

"Great. It was really great."

"Janet, dear, is this thing I am hearing about you true or not? Because I know that you don't do things of this kind."

"What is it that you have heard about me, Stacey?"

"You mean you don't know?"

"Stacey, just tell me, please. I wouldn't be asking what it is if I had heard something."

"The story about you in a hotel room in France with a cute French guy. That you had an affair with the guy …"

"What? No! Tell me that it's a joke."

"I am very serious. It's Tricia who told me about it."

"Tricia? Naomi's friend?"

"Yes. Tricia. George's ex-fiancée."

"I can't believe this. Where did Tricia get this from?"

"I don't know."

"Stacey, this is a very big lie, and I am very sure now that there is somebody out there who is jealous of me and my beautiful family and who wants to destroy my happiness because she knows that she could never

ever have a life like mine as she has already messed up her own life with her wicked heart."

"She? She? Who are you talking about?"

"Stacey, we have to be careful. I now feel how Zulu felt when she was betrayed by a friend and then another friend."

"Janet, all I know is that this whole story is one big planned lie and a trap because I know you too well, you could never do such a thing; but my concern is we have to get the person who made it all up."

"Stacey, can you come here whenever you are free? We need to talk."

"I am on my way, dear. Give me a few minutes."

"Thanks a lot."

"You are welcome, love."

A few minutes later Stacey arrived at my place. We discussed issue after issue. I told her that, besides her, the only two people who knew about my holiday were Zulu and Naomi. I said that when I was in France Naomi did not stop calling me; she must have rung every five minutes.

Stacey laughed. "I know who started this lie. But don't worry – we will catch her just in time. Let's take things slowly so that she doesn't realise that we are on to her."

Then Stacey told me about her own experience with the angels of the other side, the bad side:

She called me her 'best friend'. As she walked into my flat with her fiancé I was sitting on the sofa with my fiancé. She looked deeply into my fiancé's eyes. It was like they had met before; I was jealous. She kept looking straight into his eyes. I became very uncomfortable and even her own fiancé was uncomfortable.

I asked her, "Have you two met before?"

131

"Oh no," she replied. "Sorry, just a resemblance to somebody I know."

I offered them a seat and some drinks. Her fiancé was my fiancé's best friend. Everyone was introduced and we each talked about our lives. Our two men left for the kitchen to prepare something very nice for all of us, as they wanted to show off their cooking skills.

She told me all about herself. "I like you and I think we would get along very well."

I replied, "I guess so."

Then we all had dinner and that was how the first day went.

The next day she came back to my flat. Whenever she visited me, she never failed to ask me how my man was doing. It was very strange to me at first, but then we became close friends and I thought it was normal. She would call me every day. She brought me apples every time she visited me. She worked in a fashionable clothes shop, so she was always fashionable and sexy. She would give me gifts for no reason at all. We were friends for almost two years. One day she called me and said that she couldn't get hold of Ryan, her fiancé. His phone was off and she had to get an important message to him. She begged me for the number of my fiancé, Josh. I was only twenty years old and very naive. I said that they might not be in the same place, but she insisted, and so I gave her Josh's number, only because of how urgent she told me the matter was. That was the mistake I made. Her name was Debby. Debby started having conversations with Josh without me knowing about it. All of a sudden Josh started acting very oddly and I became worried. When I asked him what the problem was he didn't want to talk about it. My world started falling apart. This was a man I was madly in love with and I dreamt of becoming his wife. He was so cute that women never stopped glancing at him. And he once said to me that I was and would always be the key to his heart, regardless of other women's advances towards him. He used to call me five times a day but then it became one time a day. I couldn't bear it anymore, so I thought it would be good to talk to somebody I trusted. I explained everything to Debby. She felt sorry for me and told me that she was going to talk to Josh on my behalf. I was about to give her Josh's number, but she said, "Oh, don't worry. I already have it. I saved it on my phone the last time you gave it to me."

She had tricked me so badly. I was too naive to understand her game. She played with my trust and my honest heart. The next day she called me and said that she had called Josh, who'd said he was no longer interested in the relationship because he had heard some disgusting stories about me.

I said, "But why can't he tell me himself? I have been asking him what the problem is, but he won't talk to me. It's by talking that we could find out what the matter is and try to solve it."

"Well," she replied, "you know men can be a bit harsh sometimes."

I just didn't believe Debby. Josh and I had known each other for twelve good years since primary school, so he had no reason to treat me that way. He had never behaved like that before, and I started to have a feeling that somebody was behind all this mess. I wanted to find out who it was. One night I made a plan to go to Josh's place and see whatever it was that he was hiding from me. On my way to his place I prayed that the entrance door on the first floor would be open so that I wouldn't have to ring the bell to his flat. My prayer was answered. I entered and walked to the second floor. The door to his flat was open, too. I guessed he had left it open for his mystery girl. I walked in and heard him speaking in the kitchen, so I walked straight to the kitchen.

He was surprised to see me. He was on the phone with somebody. He told them that he would call them back in a minute.

"What can I do for you, Stacey?" he asked.

"Josh, is this you?" I replied.

"What are you doing here?" he shouted.

"You can't even be bothered to greet me …"

"No. Because I don't have time for you."

"You no longer have time for me; I don't recognise you anymore. What is it that we can't talk about? What have I done to you?"

"There is nothing to talk about, Stacey. When you are through with your speech, get out of my flat. As you can see, I am cooking." He looked at me like I was a mad person.

"Josh, please tell me something, please."

"Tell you something? Hell no. You are the one to tell me something."

"Josh, you know I have nothing to tell you. You just tell me, please."

"Tell you? Oh yeah, you really want to know? What good is left about you, anyway, when you go around sleeping with other men, drinking alcohol and taking drugs? Thieving from shops? So you are a thief, Stacey? I can't believe that I was in love with a thief all this time."

I was so shocked. It was like there was something so heavy in my heart that I could hardly breathe. "Josh, me a thief? Me sleeping around? Josh, you know me too well – as far back as primary school. We have known each other for twelve years. Don't tell me that you have believed untrue stories about me? Who told you all this?"

"It's not necessary to know where I got the

information from."

"What do you mean it's not necessary? Somebody is trying to stab me in the back, and you stand here doing nothing? Tell me, or I will do something stupid! I want to know who it is, Josh, because your info is not genuine. Please tell me who told you, so I can prove to you that whoever has said this is a big liar."

"Really? OK. Have you ever stolen chocolate-chip cookies before? From a supermarket? Put them straight into your bag? Huh? Are you going to deny it?"

"Listen, it wasn't me. It was Debby who took the cookies and put them in my handbag."

"Oh, so you know about it. I thought you said you were not a thief? Now get out of my house!"

"No, Josh – this is not enough reason for you to break up with me. It's better for you to tell me that you have found someone else and I would understand."

"And what about you sleeping around with other men?"

"Please, Josh, hear me out! I am not a thief, I am not a whore and I am not a drug taker! You know me, Josh. This whole thing is a lie. Somebody is trying to destroy us, can't you see?"

"I thought I knew you, but not anymore. Please just leave."

"Josh, I can feel that you are in love with someone else, but don't let her love blind you; have a good rethink about the girl you have known all your life. And if you do rethink, trust me, you won't believe in all of these lies. I love you. Please don't do this to me."

"Leave or I will call the police on you!"

"The police? Why call the police, Josh? I can't believe you."

"Listen, leave!"

"OK, fine. I will go. But I just want you to know that I have never ever cheated on you. I have always been faithful to you, I have always loved you and I still love you, but I guess it's over. Tell Debby that I said thank you for all the misery she has caused me. Bye."

"Just go!"

"And you know what, Josh? I don't think that you truly loved me. Goodbye."

So that was how it finished between us. That same night I called Debby, but she wouldn't pick up. I texted her, saying, "Thank you very much for ruining my life. Your plans have succeeded. Well done."

Then I deleted Debby's and Josh's numbers from my phone. I changed my number. I did not seek revenge but left things as they were in the belief that one day the whole truth would come out. I decided to move on with my life. It was so hard to move on. The scar in my heart took years to heal. Then one day I met Paul, who put my life back on track. After the incident with Josh I decided never ever to give my man's number to a friend. Then guess what? One day I met Ryan on the underground. He told me that he too was disappointed in Josh – how Josh, his best friend, could go out with Debby. That Josh and him were no longer friends because of the same story and that he was sorry for me. I said to him that it was OK: I had long forgotten everything. Then Ryan said something interesting – Josh had asked him if he had any contact with me and told him, if he did, to apologise to me for all that he had done. His marriage to Debby had been a mistake. Debby was a thief. She took drugs and slept around with other men, and she had cleared all the money from his bank accounts. He had divorced her, and Debby was facing a sentence in prison for theft. I wasn't surprised at all, because I knew from the beginning that Debby was a very bad girl; she would only pretend to be a good girl just to make friends with people. The sweet sexy Debby on the outside was far sweeter than she was on the inside. Ryan went on to say that he just thanked God for everything, because it should have been him who was married to the monster. I also told Ryan how I had progressed in my life and how happy I had become.

"So, Janet, I believe that there is a reason why hell and heaven both exist, and those who belong to either one must be put in their place; as for me, Debby belonged in hell. The fool only dines with the fool and the wise with the wise. I came to understand that in life you shouldn't walk with fools and wicked people, because they will only bring about your downfall. All they do is minimise to equalise. They will say lies about you just to put out the light that shines on you. Debby destroyed me, but Naomi has surely failed you. I remember telling Debby that if I had to go to hell simply because I couldn't forgive her, then so be it. After Debby I refused to have a friend until the day I met you, Janet. Just look at the age gap between me and you; I am thirteen years older than you, but you are my only trustworthy friend. You are a true friend because you have never done me wrong, and I believe that a true friend could and would never ever wrong her fellow friend."

"Oh, that's kind of you, Stacey, and very true. I am happy to have a friend like you too. We all need good friends to rely on. But, seriously, the same thing that has happened to Zulu and you is now happening to me. Stacey, I went to France to stay with my sister-in-law, and Naomi would call me every five minutes just to find out how my holiday was going. The day before I left France my sister-in-law took me to a fine restaurant in the heart of Paris where a cute guy came up to our table and asked me out. I told him that I was married. Just as we walked out of the restaurant Naomi called me again, and I told her about the guy just to have some fun with her, since she is so crazy about cute guys. I said to her that she had just missed one cute guy and that was all. But I couldn't have imagined that she would twist the story just because she is so jealous of me."

"Well, now you have learnt your lesson. Know who to make friends with. Not everybody who wants to be your friend is genuine. Most of them just want to know who you are and will start gossiping to others about your life. All they seek is to put out the light that shines upon you, because you shine so bright that you light up the people around you. And one more thing, Janet. You need to listen to your husband when he tells you something about somebody. Don't doubt him, because husbands like yours are very honest people. As to how we are going to catch that wicked witch, this is what we are going to do ... Wait for your husband to tell you whether he has heard the rumour too. As soon as he tells you about it, let me know so that we can execute the plan. OK?"

"Thanks a lot, Stacey. I feel a lot better now. God bless you."

"You are welcome, love."

Then Stacey left.

When my husband came back from work I exercised my duty as always, but I noticed that he was not himself. He was not talking to me as he usually did. He wouldn't even look at me as we ate at the table. We didn't even watch TV together as we usually did. He went to bed very early. I followed him to bed, asking him what was wrong. He said that everything was fine. I insisted that he wasn't alright, but he wouldn't tell me anything. I prayed to God that night that my husband would tell me something before he left for work the following morning.

That night I couldn't sleep. I was so emotional. I

couldn't believe the lies about me that were coming from people. Thank God I was with my sister-in-law, who could testify for me. Imagine if I had been alone. The same thing that had happened to Zulu and Stacey was now happening to me. So these bad angels, as I had always called them, were everywhere, like I had always thought. You couldn't tell who they were until you got to know them.

My husband called me into the living room the next morning and asked me to sit down. "What is this story I am hearing about you and a French man in a hotel room in France?"

"Me with a French guy? No, that can't be true. I mean, it's not true."

"You don't listen to me when I tell you that your friend Naomi is not a good friend, do you?"

"What about Naomi again?"

"Anyway, you have nothing to do with all this, right?"

"Honey, you know your wife. I know nothing about this. I don't know who's behind it, but all I know – which you also know yourself – is that I went to France to see your sister. I remember your sister and I went to a restaurant where this man came up to our table and asked me out. I told him that I was married. Your sister was there and she can testify to this. I later told Naomi about it just to have fun with her because she fancies cute-looking guys. That was all. I don't know how and why the story has been changed into something else."

"It is OK. I trust you and I believe what you have just told me. But can you just stop seeing Naomi, please?"

"It's a promise, honey. I will stop being her friend."

"Alright, my sugar. Love you."

"Love you too, honey."

As soon as my husband left for work I thought it

was the best time to call Stacey so we could execute our plan. I had to execute the plan because I wanted to prove my innocence to my husband as Stacey said. After I had called Stacey, she said that she would come to my house at 6 p.m. that evening. And that was what she did.

She started reminding me how the plan was to work. Ten minutes later my husband walked in. Again he was in a bad mood, as if he had heard something again. He greeted us and dropped his phone on the coffee table and went off to the bathroom to take his shower. Stacey and I continued talking about our plan. Then my husband's phone started ringing. It rang five times. The number was not registered to his contact list. Stacey and I became curious. Then a text message came in.

I said, "I don't like what I am about to do, but I have to do it. I have to check who it is."

For the very first time I checked my husband's phone. There were five missed calls from a number not registered in his phone and a text message, which said: "You have to believe me. Your wife is cheating on you and this is not the first time she has done it."

I was shocked. I felt like something heavy was covering my chest and I couldn't breathe. Stacey told me to calm down and take a deep breath; it was time for us to act. As we waited for my husband, Stacey asked me to call that number with my own mobile phone without letting the line ring. As soon as I pressed the 'call' button, the name came out on the screen as 'Naomi'. I quickly ended the call. I couldn't believe my eyes. My whole world was being torn apart. I was falling down from a very high mountain. I became very angry, but Stacey asked for my patience. When my husband had finished his shower and had his dinner, he came to tell us that he was very tired and needed to sleep. Stacey begged him for a few minutes of his time, saying that there was something we all had to discuss. Stacey then explained the whole situation.

"John, I am here this evening for one main purpose: to track down the person who is trying to destroy your marriage. I just want you to cooperate with me, please. I know that you are not used to this type of game, but please just assist us. I know you are a very honourable man and I apologise for any inconvenience that this may cause, but it is important that you do what I am about to ask you. Thank you."

The plan was that we would each call Naomi on speaker phone, pretending that we were in different places.

John: "What is it that you want me to do? I am all ears."

Stacey: "John, I have come to notice that Naomi is trying to destroy your marriage, and I am here to track her down and prove your wife's innocence."

John: "Good that you have noticed that too … I have been telling my wife about this all this time, but she wouldn't listen to me, and now look at where we are."

Me: "Honey, I am sorry. I know that I have been stubborn in not listening to you, but I promise that it won't happen again."

Stacey: "Yes, I know, John, and that is where she went wrong. Anyway, I am going to proceed with the execution of the plan. You both watch me first – then it will be Janet's turn. I am going to call Tricia and put her on speaker."

Stacey called Tricia and put her on the loud speaker so we could all listen to the conversation.

"Hello, Tricia."

"Oh, hi Stacey. How do you do?"

"I am very fine. And you, dear?"

"I'm good. So what's up?"

"Nothing much … Eh-eh, Tricia, I just wanted to find out if the story you told me about Janet and a French man in a hotel is really true."

"Well, to be honest with you, I don't know. I was just asked by Naomi to spread the news around, but I am not sure myself."

"So Naomi is the one who told you the story?"

"Yep."

"I see."

"Is there any problem?"

"Yes, there is a problem – the story is causing a huge amount of damage to Janet's marriage and her reputation."

"I am really sorry. Naomi asked me to do this."

"Tricia, you don't do such things even when you are being asked to. It's not nice; it's very wicked."

"I am sorry, Stacey. I will call Janet to tell her how sorry I am."

"Well, you'd better be sorry, but for now I have to hang up. Thank you and bye for now."

Then Stacey called Naomi.

"Hi Naomi."

"Oh, Stacey, how are you?"

"I'm very fine, thank you. And you?"

"I'm alright. Just home doing nothing."

"Oh, I see. Naomi, there is this thing I have been wanting to ask you if you don't mind."

"Yeah, sure, go on. What is it?"

"Do you know the story that has been going around about Janet and the French guy in a hotel in Paris?"

"Yeah, I do."

"Who said it? I mean, who started it?"

"Well, nobody did. I was there myself."

"I see. OK, that was all. I just wanted to know the source of the information; I thought Tricia was lying."

"No, it's true. I was the one who told Tricia about

142

it."

"OK, dear. Thank you and have a good evening. Bye."

"Bye."

I cried when Stacey got off the phone. How could Naomi lie like that? What for? What had I ever done to her that would make her hurt me that badly?

Then Stacey told me that it was my turn to call Naomi.

"Hello Naomi."

"Hey, Janet, baby girl. How are you?"

"I am not fine, Naomi."

"What's wrong, my dear friend?"

"My roof is on fire."

"What? What do you mean?"

"My husband is accusing me of cheating on him. Somebody told him about me and a French guy in a hotel …"

"No. That can't possibly be true."

"Yes, Naomi. He's accusing me of committing adultery and intends to divorce me."

"Wait, let me get this right. Your husband is accusing you of adultery and is intending to divorce you?"

"Yes, Naomi, and I don't know what to do."

"Well, I personally know that you couldn't possibly have done that. You are a very honest and faithful woman."

"Tell me, Naomi … My husband doesn't know me anymore. I am going crazy. I can't do this on my own. I need your help. Can you talk to him for me, please? I can't do this on my own. Come and tell him that it's all lies. Perhaps somebody jealous of me is trying to destroy our marriage."

"Calm down, Janet, darling. Don't cry, please. Stop crying, OK? Your husband must be very stupid to have listened to such untrue stories about you. A woman like you could never cheat on her husband. Who could be behind all this?"

"I don't know, Naomi. I heard that the whole story came from Tricia."

"Tricia! That stupid jealous girl! She will never change."

"Naomi, please just come now. Please. I can't bear this any longer."

"OK, I will come … Is your husband home with you?"

"No. We quarrelled and he has just left. He said he's not coming back until tomorrow."

"That's a pity, but let me tell you that he is the one who is cheating on you. Go ahead with the divorce. Anyway, let me come over so we can sort this out. I will be right there. Give me five minutes and I will be there."

"Please hurry up, Naomi. Bye."

I went mad. Naomi had changed her story with me. I was in tears. I couldn't believe what was happening to me. Naomi was very wicked.

Then it was my husband's turn to call Naomi.

"Hello, John, darling. Wow! For the very first time you have called me. I hope all is well?"

"How can all be well when you have been calling me and texting me all this time to tell me these stories about my wife? Now to be honest with you I need one last confirmation from you, because I don't ever want to regret what I am about to do."

"Well well well … first of all I have been telling you all this because I care for you. You are such a lovely person, and you don't deserve to be cheated on."

"Naomi, please stop the drama and just be honest with me. This is not the first time you have told me that my wife is a cheater. You once told me that she kissed a guy at Tricia's birthday party, then that she tried to seduce your boyfriend, Kevin, and now that she has had an affair with a French man. I mean, are all these stories true or lies? Or could you be lying out of jealousy?"

"Me, jealous of Janet? For what? Hell no! What does she have that I don't have? I am a woman and she is a woman, too. The stories are true. In fact, they are very true, my darling, because I was there myself. I mean, I was with her myself when she did it."

"Did what?"

"When she left for the hotel room with the guy."

"How did it happen that you both happened to be at the same hotel? Wasn't she with my sister, Esther?"

"I don't know if she was with your sister, but she phoned me on that day to accompany her there."

"But Naomi, wasn't it the same day you came to visit me here at home and tried to seduce me? How come you happened to be there at the hotel?"

"OK, OK. Confession – it was Tricia who told me about it."

"And how did Tricia get to know about it?"

"I don't know. Tricia is Janet's friend, too, isn't she?"

"Sure, of course she is Janet's friend, too. Tell me, Naomi. What do you want from me? Let us come to an understanding, and I want you to be honest with yourself – do you fancy me? Or is it just that you are jealous of Janet's happiness?"

"Me, jealous of that …? Whatever. I have already told you that I am not jealous of her. Can you please stop talking of jealousy?"

"What did you mean by 'me, jealous of that …' You didn't finish your sentence."

"Well, if you don't know, your wife is too proud of herself. I mean, she should slow down a bit, because she is not the only pretty woman in the whole wide world. She's too confident in herself. Anyway, all I know is that the story is true. That's what Tricia told me. And to answer your question of whether I like you? John, I am in love with you. You are the perfect man and any woman would want to have you."

"On the contrary – my wife is very humble. Maybe it's you who can't stand her. Listen, could we go somewhere and talk about this?"

"You mean today?"

"I mean now."

"Sure, of course! Ah-ah-ah!" she shouted with joy.

"Alright, let's meet up somewhere. I will text you the place and time after I have figured out where it will be. Keep your phone with you, as you will be receiving a text from me in a few minutes. Is that OK by you?"

"Of course, honey. Cannot wait to see you so I can cool down your heart. By the way, are you home?"

"No, I am not. You just wait for my text."

"Alright, sweetie."

"OK, bye for now."

"Bye, honey. Kiss."

John hung up. I cried and cried. What a demon I had as a friend. So she had loved my husband all this time.

Stacey told me to call Naomi again, and so we spoke with the conversation on speaker phone, as before.

"Naomi, where are you?"

"Baby girl, I am on my way; but I won't stay long because I have somewhere else to go."

"Come on, Naomi. I thought you were helping me solve this matter?"

"Yes, I am, but I won't stay for long, OK? But I am on my way."

"Never mind. It doesn't matter how long you will or will not stay, as long as we find a solution to this problem."

146

"OK, see you in a bit."

I just couldn't believe what was happening to me – so Naomi had been to my house while I was away in France to try to seduce my husband. I went mad. I just couldn't wait to deal with her. I was anxious. Just five minutes passed before the doorbell rang. As I opened the door Naomi held my face to her arms and kissed my forehead, saying, "I love you, Janet, and I would never let anything bad happen to you. You are my best friend. I am sorry for all that's happening, but we will definitely find a solution to it, OK? So wipe away your tears."

I couldn't wait to get my head off the devil's hands. "Let's go to the living room and talk, please."

As soon as we entered the living room she couldn't believe her eyes. The three people she had just spoken to on the phone had actually been calling her from the same place. She became speechless.

"Oh h-e-l-l-o John ... S-t-a-c-e-y, so you are here ... eh-eh," she stammered.

I guess I wasn't very patient. "You daughter of Satan! You are surprised to see my husband at home, aren't you? You are very bad, Naomi! So you have had the nerve to be calling my husband all this time? Who are you to be calling him, and who asked you to do so? And how did you get his number?"

"Janet, please calm down. I can explain things. I took it from your mobile phone the day you gave birth. Yes, it was that day," she trembled.

"So when I asked you that day to call my husband so that he could bring me some apples, you used that opportunity to get hold of his number? You are a real scorpion, Naomi!"

"You are such a bitch, Naomi!" said Stacey. "Daughter of the devil!"

Naomi started to panic. "Please, Stacey. Take it easy

on me."

I was furious with her. "Who's going to take it easy on you when you have been the scorpion biting me all this time? You have no shame at all … trying to seduce my husband. Now get the hell out of my house! Now!"

"Janet, please – I am so sorry. I guess I was out of my mind," she sobbed.

"You have always been out of your mind, Naomi. You called me your best friend, yet you have hurt me so badly. How can you claim to dearly love a friend and yet be the first to destroy her life? No one can do what you have done to me and not be a hypocrite. This friendship is over and over for good. Now get out!"

"Janet, please." She fell to her knees. "It was the demon in me."

Stacey shouted at her to get out.

"Please, you guys should try to understand me. I am not as bad as you think. OK, Janet, yes, it was me who made up the story. I came to envy your happiness so much. I wanted to settle down, too," she sobbed.

Stacey was incredulous. "Settle down with Janet's husband? You must be crazy, Naomi! You are a fool, an idiot – in fact, you are a monster! Can't you find a husband of your own? Leave this house now! And close the door behind you!"

Naomi left my house. As soon as she closed the door I felt peace again in my home. My happiness was restored. My heart was relieved. I could breathe again. That was how the friendship with the monster ended. I thanked Stacey for everything. Stacey was a good and true friend because a true friend would never ever hurt her fellow friend. Before Stacey left she warned my husband and me never to let anything like this happen to our marriage again. She told me never to doubt my husband again and said that I should listen to him when he told me something about somebody. I was very thankful to Stacey for proving my innocence to my husband.

After Stacey had left, I asked my husband for forgiveness. "Honey, I am so sorry for not believing you all this time."

"It's OK, sugar. I am only glad that the mystery has been solved. Just be more careful with friends from now onwards. Man can make your success, but man can also destroy your life. So be very careful when choosing your friends. You must seek friends who will bring something more to your life and not those who will take from it. When a friend truly loves you, they respect you and **everything you are** (your property/home, lifestyle, family, money, etc.). Bad people can never form a good friendship/relationship. They never have true love for you – their love for you is for materialistic or physical interest and not for spiritual interest. As soon as they break you, they are gone. They become so jealous when they find out that you are good. They start envying what you have and long to have it for themselves, and so they wait for an opportunity to destroy you so they can take what belongs to you or just laugh at you and be happy with the fact that you have lost all you had."

"Honey, I thank God for giving me a husband like you. What if you had fallen into Naomi's traps? What would have happened to us?"

"Well, that would never have happened, because I am John, and I am different from the other men she has destroyed."

"I love you so very much, honey."

"Love you too, sugar. Just listen to me next time. And please add this for me to your book: *What a wise person standing on a mountain can see coming up the river, you who are standing at the river cannot see. That's why many people don't know what is around them and often make many mistakes until they get to the mountain and stand where the wise man is standing. Then they can see what the wise man saw coming. So if you are at the river, you need to listen to what the wise man is shouting out at you and telling you is coming."*

"I surely will add this, my love."

Chapter 9

Tricia would not stop calling me. One day she called me seven times, but still I wouldn't answer. She left a voicemail which said, "I know you don't want to pick up my calls, but I just want to say sorry for every wrong I have caused you. Please forgive me, Janet."

She texted me, saying, "Sorry for all the trouble that Naomi has made me cause you. Please forgive me. I never intended hurting you. I have learnt from my wrongdoings."

I texted her back: "You become a fool when you dine with a fool. Never text or call my number again."

But still Tricia did not stop calling me and texting me. I even thought of changing my number, but many good friends had my number, and I didn't want to change it just because of Naomi and Tricia.

Two weeks later, around 1 p.m. on a Monday, my seventeen-month-old daughter and I were in the living room. My daughter was watching CBeebies while I was on the computer writing another story for my book. Then I felt like eating blueberry muffins, so I decided to go and bake some in the kitchen. My daughter and I were big fans of blueberry muffins; we baked them nearly every day. As soon as I stepped into the kitchen my mobile phone started ringing. I had left it in the living room, so I went back to collect it and then returned to the kitchen. The missed call was from Tricia. I didn't want to ring her back. She called again and again. There turned out to be twenty missed calls from her.

Then somebody was banging on the door. I wondered why the person had not thought to ring the doorbell. The person banged and banged so hard. This was very unusual. I thought that it might possibly be the postman with a parcel, but still, why couldn't he ring the bell?

I went to see who it was. As I got close to the door I heard a voice say, "Open the fucking door, Janet!"

I was fairly sure that it was Naomi. My kitchen window was open and I could hear loud noise coming from outside. Then a text came to my mobile, but I wouldn't check it. I rushed back to the kitchen to see if it was really her. From my kitchen window it was possible to see who was at the door.

It was definitely her. I shouted back, "What are you doing at my door, Naomi? Haven't I made it clear to you that we are no longer friends?"

"Just open the fucking door, Janet. I need to talk to you!"

"Talk to me about what, Naomi?"

"Listen, Janet, I love you so much. I loved you the very first time I set eyes on you. I have always been obsessed with you. Please, let's talk! I miss your friendship! Can't you see that I am fucking crazy about you, Janet?"

"You must be out of your mind. Go and see a psychiatrist and leave me alone!"

"Open the fucking door before I lose it! Damn it!"

I rushed to the living room to get my daughter. I was scared and did not know what Naomi was up to.

"Are you there, Janet? Open this door before I do something stupid!" she shouted.

"What do you want from me? Just go away!"

"Alright then, I am coming through the backyard. Don't you worry, I will jump the fence!"

"And I will call the police! Just go away! You are causing a nuisance to the neighbourhood!"

She did go through the backyard. I could see her jump the fence from the living room, because we have a glass back door that faces the garden. She looked like a depressed mental person. In her right hand she was holding a kitchen knife. I quickly picked up my mobile phone. She came closer to the back door and tried to open it, but thank God it was locked.

She shouted again: "Open this door, Janet! Now!"

"Go away!" I shouted as I walked back into the living room.

"Open it or I will break the glass! I mean it!"

"And I will call the police!"

"You wouldn't call the police on me, would you, my queen of beauty? You are too soft-hearted to do that. Listen, Janet, all I want us to do is talk. I want to apologise to you for all the trouble I have caused you and at the same time tell you how much I love you. OK, if it's for the knife, I am dropping it down now. See? I have dropped it. So open the door for me, Janet. Please."

"You must be stupid to think I will open the door to you, even when you have no weapon with you. All I want you to do is leave my house now! Because, trust me, I am calling the police straight away!"

She picked up the sharp long knife and started pointing it at me. I took my mobile phone and called my husband instead of the police. But he was not picking up. I called again and again but still he did not answer. I feared for my life and that of my daughter.

Then my husband called back.

"Hello sugar, is everything alright? I had ten missed calls from you."

"Honey, Naomi is in our backyard, threatening our lives."

"What? Have you called the police?"

"I wanted to see how bad she would get first."

"Call the police now! You don't wait in situations like this. I am on my way. Stay on the phone with me, and use the landline to call the police. Where is Erica?"

"I have got her with me."

"Good! Keep her close to you and shut all the doors and windows. I am on my way."

I then checked the text message that I hadn't wanted to check in the first place – it was from Tricia and said, "Don't open the door, Naomi is coming to harm you."

Naomi was still there, shouting. She got worse. She was knocking her head on the back door and trying to break the glass with her foot. I called the police straight away.

"There is somebody in my garden with a long sharp knife, threatening to harm me and my daughter. I fear for our lives."

I was asked for my address. The police got there within ten minutes. That was a great relief. My house was surrounded by police. Three policemen went to the garden while some came into the house through the front door and some stayed outside. Those who went to the garden arrested Naomi and took the knife off her. Just a few minutes later my husband got home too. I said to the police officers who were inside with me that I wanted to see Naomi before she went with them because I had something to tell her. I told Naomi that the good and the bad could never be friends, while she shouted at the police officers, "I know my rights, I know my rights …"

One police officer told her, "I am arresting you for assault and trespass into somebody's property. You have the right to remain silent. Anything you say could be used against you in a court of law."

I couldn't believe that this was happening to me. We usually see these things in movies, but to me it became a reality. What could make somebody want to harm another person for no reason at all? I came to realise that what Stacey told me about jealousy was true.

Stacey once told me something about jealousy:
Jealousy

Jealousy is a very bad thing; it destroys families, relationships and friendships.

Jealousy comes when someone is set against another because that other person has something which he or she does not have. Such things might include beauty, intelligence, good behaviour, good friends, love, happiness, peace, money or righteousness.

But why would some people be against others for these reasons? Is it just because they do not have a good heart, or is it because they find themselves too inferior to others?

If someone is not particularly attractive to other people, yet finds out that his friend or relative is attractive, he has a choice. If he is a good person and knows that he can also be attractive, he will not be concerned about the attractiveness of his friend and will not think of doing him harm. Instead he will try to make himself attractive too. If he is a bad person in the same situation, he might do something to destroy the attractiveness of his friend or relative. He might do this by inventing lies and setting traps for him. They even go beyond their jealousy to kill.

I had to call Zulu and Stacey to tell them the whole story. Later on Zulu did something very funny to respond to what Naomi did to me. Zulu posted something on Naomi's Facebook wall; it was a funny short story. More than two hundred people liked this and it received over a hundred comments. It was as if I had not been Naomi's only victim. There were hundreds of us. As I read through the story, I guessed Naomi deserved it.

It is not everything you see that you try

Lionel was an eleven-year-old boy. He was calm and gentle. He did not talk a lot, but his gentleness caused him humiliation and provoked conflict between him and his mates, who saw him as being cowardly.

One day, Lionel was on his way home from school when a group of ten of his friends attacked him as they often did. They began to insult him, saying that it would only take a slap to kill him. On top of the insults they threatened him, saying, "Move if you are a man. If you move you will walk home naked."

Lionel did not move. He stood there encircled by them and said, "Guys, let me go home. I do not want a fight."

They answered with, "A fight? Do you think you can fight us?"

The leader of the group was Terry, who said, "Poor Lionel. Do you think you can fight me, Tall Terry the Tiger That Ties and Terrifies?"

"No, I cannot. That is why I beg you to let me go," responded Lionel.

"If you want me to let you go home, you should first call me chief," said Terry.

"Chief," said Lionel.

"Now jump," said Terry.

Lionel jumped.

"Now cry," said Terry.

Lionel refused, firmly saying that he would not do that.

"Oh yeah, Lionel Bin?" said Terry, while the other friends laughed.

"My name is not Lionel Bin. My name is Lionel Elliot," said Lionel.

"Oh, don't worry, I will tell you why I called you

156

Lionel Bin. Do you see the rubbish bin right over there? That is where you will find yourself in just a second," said Terry.

Terry started to show off. He slapped Lionel five times on his cheeks. Lionel turned red, touched his face and said, "Please, Terry, let me go."

Terry then punched Lionel to the floor and started kicking him.

Lionel pleaded with him. "Let me go home, Terry, please!"

When Terry was about to give Lionel a final kick, Lionel became a lion and scratched Terry's face. The other friends ran. Lionel stood up to Terry, saying, "I am Lionel, the Living Lion, your chief. I am the chief of the jungle. I will not kill you, but I will teach you a lesson."

Tall Terry the Tiger That Ties and Terrifies was crying and apologising to him. Lionel, king of the jungle, returned to his normal self and walked away, leaving Terry with a few words. "It is not everything you see that you try. Good evening."

Chapter 10

A month later Zulu called me to tell me that she had passed her GCSEs and had applied for her AGCEs, also called A levels. I was very happy for her. She was working very hard to realise her dreams, and I became happier for her when she told me that things were moving on very well between her and Spencer, and they had got engaged.

Stacey became pregnant and I was very happy for her. I became pregnant too. My life became happier than ever. I finished my book and it was ready for publication.

Nine months passed. I was in hospital giving birth to my twins. My mum and dad were there with me, my husband too. I gave birth to twins: a boy and a girl. I was amazed at all the blessings God was pouring on me, but I deserved them all.

A few hours later I couldn't believe my eyes: it was Stacey, Zulu and Tricia. I wondered what Tricia was doing with them. I didn't want to see her, so I said, "No, don't come and spoil my day."

My mum said that I should go easy on myself, as I had just given birth. I said to my mum, "Not until that lady is out of this place."

Then Stacey said, "Janet, I am sorry to have brought Tricia with us. I know that you are not happy to see us come with her, but she begged us to bring her here. She said that she had to see you. We didn't know what to do. We did warn her that you wouldn't want to see her."

I told Tricia to say what she had to say and then to leave.

This was what she had to say: "Janet, I am truly sorry for everything. Sorry for the 'hotel story' I spread all over the place. It was because Naomi asked me to do so. She wanted to ruin your good reputation because she had always been jealous of you. She wanted to take over you ..."

"And you did it, didn't you?" I replied.

"Yes, I did, but I later realised that what I did was wrong. That's why I have always been wanting to make things up to you."

"You people have no conscience, no manners, and no morals at all. You are like demons ..."

"Please, Janet, I am a changed person now. I am telling you the truth. I stopped being friends with Naomi the day you and Stacey trapped her at your house. I told her that she was now on her own. I came to realise that the type of life Naomi and I were living was not the right life to live, and the things we were doing were not the right things to do, so I stopped being her friend. I am really working hard to make things better for myself. I have really changed. I know I have wronged you, but please forgive me. I have come to understand that true friends are very hard to find – meaning I have not been able to find a good friend like you, Janet. You know that Naomi even insisted that I accompany her on the day she came to attack you, but I refused, because I realised that she was a very bad person, and I told her that I was not going with her. I tried calling you to let you know that she was coming to harm you, but you wouldn't pick up your phone, so that's why I texted you. I no longer go about destroying other people's happiness. You don't get many chances in life to make it up to yourself, so I really wanted to move on to the other side of life, the good side. I mean I am now an angel of the other side, the good side."

"OK. It's good to hear that. It's good that you have learnt some good lessons and I am happy to hear that you have changed, because I have always been of the opinion that people can change their ways of living. I forgave you a long time ago, but unfortunately we cannot be friends anymore, because you don't get to trust a lion that has attempted to kill you twice – even if it comes around you smoothly to make up. See, Tricia, you can never tell what goes on in the heart of a man. Sorry, dear, but that's how it is."

"It's OK, Janet. Thank you very much for your comprehension. Before I leave I would love to congratulate you on your twins by giving you this gift card. Please take it. Inside the card I have written something down. If you publish your book one day, will you please add this to your book as a way of forgiving me?"

"I will see to that."

"Thank you. God bless. Bye."

"Bye, and thanks for the gift card. God bless you too."

And that was how I finally stopped Tricia from being my friend again. Later I opened the gift card. This was what she had written:

It is hard to find someone kind

Many people are truly kind from the bottom of their heart. They give help and love without expecting any reward and without talking behind your back. They do not play tricks on you. Such people are blessed because they are true.

Many other people are kind, but not from the bottom of their heart. They pretend to give help and to love but do not really mean it. Once you turn your back, they talk about you. Most of them expect a reward or they might use you, or have an interest in you. Such people are not blessed because they are not true.

Today you have friends and will continue to make friends in the future, but I suggest that you should be careful. Do not think he is kind just because your friend has given you bread. It is hard to find someone kind; among fifty people we may find only one truly kind person.

The next day I was discharged from hospital. On my way home with my parents and husband I was surprised to see what was awaiting me at home. As we walked into the house there was a big party going on with some beautiful music playing. There was a lot of food and drinks. Stacey and her husband were there, Zulu and Spencer too, my husband's friends from work and my parents' friends. I asked my husband what was going on. He replied with a great smile, "It's a party for you and the twins – a way of thanking you for bringing two new beautiful angels into our lives."

So it was a party for me and the twins. Amazing, isn't it? My parents always said, "Good things come only to those who are good." And you know what? Yep, they were right!

Ever since my life has been happy and happier every day!

THE END

Get to know your friends through words and actions to tell how real they are.

A true man is a man who knows or must know what is around him but who lives according to his principles.